HOT SEAL, BOURBON NEAT

SEALS IN PARADISE

PARKER KINCADE

DEDICATION

To my brother, Dave. For all the bottles we've shared and those we've yet to open. Thank you for having the patience of a saint when it comes to a pesky sister with a bazillion military questions.

To the SEALs in Paradise authors: I am humbled and honored to be among you.

And to Asher. Told you frolicking could be fun!

1

PARADISE.

Asher "Knots" Dillon snorted to himself and raised the highball glass to his lips. The yellowish liquid barely resembled bourbon, but, hey, what did he expect from the land of rum and froufrou drinks?

The weather on Grand Turks was a balmy eighty-five degrees, the sun so bright he squinted behind his Oakleys. He took a healthy gulp, swirling the alcohol around his tongue until his tastebuds burned in protest. It really was horrible bourbon.

Christ. How the hell had he ended up here?

"Ash! Come on!"

Oh, right. Because his mom and sixteen-year old sister had planned this little vacay, and if being a Navy SEAL had taught him anything, it was that there was no fucking way the two most important women in his life were leaving the United States without protection. His mom, smart woman that she was, predicted his reaction and had booked a suite for him as well.

So, here he was. On leave at the Midnight Bay Beach

Resort in Turks and Caicos, where vacationers let loose, drank fruity drinks with ridiculous little adornments, and frolicked in the waves. *Frolicked*, for fuck's sake. Didn't people understand how dangerous the ocean could be? Oh, sure, it looked innocent enough, but Asher knew better than anyone that looks could be deceiving. Rip currents, shorebreaks, sharks—there were a thousand things that could go wrong when a person entered the water.

Asher cringed as he took another sip of the rotgut. He wasn't being fair. The general population wasn't being dumped into the middle of the ocean in the dead of night with a hundred pounds of gear strapped to their bodies. He got that. In his defense, any man who made it through Hell Week of BUD/S training lost some, if not all, love for the water. Any SEAL who said differently was a motherfucking liar. The ocean wasn't designed for recreation. It was deep and treacherous, with a mood that could change from calm to hell-on-earth in the space of a heartbeat.

And don't even get him started on the beach. His team had done enough time in the Gobi Desert that Asher swore he was still sweating sand out of his skin, months later.

His idea of a good time, this was not. Give him mountains and snow and a decent goddamn glass of bourbon...

Asher sighed.

Maybe next year.

"Asher!" Gracie bellowed again, drawing out his name as only a teenager could.

As he raised a hand to wave an *I see you. Carry on, preferably without me* to Gracie, he caught movement out of the corner of his eye. He glanced over in time to see a woman at a table not far from him surge to her feet. From his position behind her, Asher couldn't help but appreciate the view. Her light-colored hair was pulled into a ponytail. It ruffled in the breeze, teasing the golden skin between her shoulder blades. Her bathing suit was a one-piece that left her back exposed to the lower curve. And oh, what a back it was. Sleek and soft looking, with muscles that moved with elegant efficiency. She wore one of those oversized scarf-wrap things around her hips, but he could see enough of her legs to know she didn't need heels to give her the illusion of delicious length. She had it in spades.

Asher spent the day tossing out warning vibes to anyone who approached like they were beads at Mardi Gras, but if this woman had interrupted his solitude, he might've been inclined to ask her to join him. In his room. Naked.

"I'm good, thanks," the woman said, making Asher wonder what question he'd missed. Her voice had a vaguely familiar quality. Smooth as silk, with a steely-edged finish that caused a trail of pleasure to skirt down his spine.

He gave himself permission to revel in the sensation. Work kept him so busy lately that he'd neglected meeting any need that wasn't required to keep him alive. Now that he was on leave, he might have to see to his other, more carnal, needs.

"I've got a private cabana down the beach." The words dripped with innuendo, drawing Asher's attention away from the pretty lady to the guy standing in front of her. A surfer-blond college type. No more than twenty, twenty-one, tops. Fucking frat boy if Asher had ever seen one.

He looked like the other male vacationers on the beach with his bare chest and brightly colored board shorts. His head of messy curls needed a good shearing, and his expression was more leer than smile. The determined look in the frat boy's eyes said he wouldn't take no lightly. The way his friends were offering encouragement from a table close by proved the point.

Damn it. Was it too much to ask to enjoy his shitty bourbon in peace?

To her credit, the woman didn't back down. "No, thank you. As I said before, I'm fine right here."

"Oh, you're definitely fine." Frat boy's friends cheered and he tossed them a thumbs up.

Really, douche? No means no. Back away.

"I'm also definitely busy. I have work to do." She tried to step around him, but frat boy followed, squaring off with her. "If I could just..."

Frat boy spread his skinny arms. "Who works at the beach?"

"I do."

"Take a break then. Come on, sweet cheeks. Let's have some fun." Frat boy tipped a colorful girly drink to his lips. Not all of the slush made it into his mouth, though. He wiped away the portion sliding down his chin and then smeared it against his stomach with a smarmy grin.

"Want a taste of my drink? It's delicious."

Cue more laughter from the table o' asshole. A few of them high-fived.

Classy. Their parents should be so proud.

Asher couldn't take much more of this shit. Someone needed to teach these assholes some respect.

He glanced away long enough to check on his mom. She was right where Asher had left her, stretched out on a lounge chair with her nose in a book. He scanned the water for Gracie. It took him less than a minute to catch sight of her. Gracie bobbed and danced in the waves with a group of girls, her expression alight with youth and happiness. If Asher had his way, Gracie would never know anything but whatever she was feeling in that moment. He wasn't naive enough to believe he could shield her from the harshness of the world, but that didn't mean he wouldn't try.

Satisfied his mom was safe and Gracie wasn't falling prey to fucktard frat boys, Asher refocused on the activity within the beachside bar.

The kid hadn't given up.

"One drink," he begged.

"I'm sorry. Thank you for the offer, but I-I'm meeting someone."

Asher chuckled against the rim of his glass, liking her gumption. But if she wanted to be convincing about meeting someone, she shouldn't have made it sound as if she'd just had the greatest idea in the history of ideas. The little minx wasn't meeting anyone. She had just told one of those little white lies women used to get out of uncomfortable situations. Not that Asher blamed her. Frat boy was an ass.

The woman moved to step around frat boy again, and again the kid blocked her way.

"Excuse me. I need to order drinks for us. Not for you and me, us," she clarified. "Me and him, us. So, please. Let me by."

Frat boy reached out. The woman tried to bat his hand away, but frat boy dodged her attempt and latched on. Asher zeroed in on the fingers that curled into her golden skin and his blood pressure went on the rise. Persistence, however futile, was one thing. Touching was quite another.

Frat boy swayed his hips with the worst dirty dance move Asher had ever had the misfortune to witness.

"I've got drinks in my cabana." Frat boy licked his lips, his glance dropping to, Asher assumed, ogle the woman's tits. "Your friend can come. I don't mind sharing."

Frat boy clamped his other hand around her wrist and tugged her in close. Her audible gasp sealed the kid's fate.

"In fact..." Frat boy waved a come hither to some of his buddies. "I'll bring some friends, too. We'll make it a party."

Oh, you want to party, motherfucker?

Asher downed the rest of the bourbon and slid from the barstool.

Welcome to fucking paradise.

"Look..." The woman's voice was a mixture of exasperation and annoyance.

"Brett."

"Look, *Brett*. I appreciate the offer, but I really must decline." The last words were annoyingly polite, but pushed through clenched teeth. "I don't have time for this. I have work to do and my, um ... my boyfriend will be here any minute."

"Boyfriend?"

Frat boy really was daft. And he never saw Asher coming.

With a strike worthy of a cobra, Asher's hand engulfed Brett's forearm. He squeezed in just the right spot and...

"Ow! What the hell man!"

Brett's fingers shot open, releasing the woman with a reflexive jerk.

"I do believe the lady said no. If you're unfamiliar with the word, I'd be happy to give you a crash course."

"Who the fuck are you?"

Seemed frat boy hadn't bought her boyfriend story either. Asher released the kid with a little shove. "I'm the guy who's going to beat your sorry ass to a pulp if you don't step off."

Asher caught movement from the asshole table and

raised a palm toward Brett's buddies. "Stay where you are," he commanded, the transition from beach bum to SEAL as easy as breathing. "You don't want any of this."

Surprisingly enough, they heeded his warning. Seemed Brett's friends weren't as dumb as their buddy.

With the immediate threat averted, Asher finally turned his attention to the woman standing next to him. Eyes the color of frosted sapphires met his. His lungs heaved as recognition hit like a two-by-four to the gut.

Holy shit.

He would know those eyes anywhere. They'd been haunting his dreams, his fantasies, for years. It was *her*. Brooke Ramsey. His partner in a one-night stand that lasted for a glorious, sex-filled month. God, what had it been? Eight years?

Brooke's recollection was a split second behind his. Gratitude melted in a fiery blaze. If those icy blues could've shot laser beams, Asher would be dead where he stood. And maybe he was, because he never thought he'd see her again on this side of the pearly gates. That had been the plan anyway.

He almost couldn't believe it.

Asher shifted closer, hungry to take her in. She was still a beauty. Her hair wasn't just blonde. The wavy mass contained a plethora of yellow, gold, and red strands that glittered in the sun. Her striking eyes had golden lashes that wouldn't quit. She had delicate girl-next-door features, highlighted by an array of adorable freckles that dotted her nose and cheeks.

God, he'd missed those freckles.

Asher opened his mouth to ask if she was okay and instead heard himself say, "Hey, sweetheart. Sorry I'm late."

Brooke's smile was tight as she took a step back, then another, putting distance between them.

"Your timing couldn't be better, *babe*." Oh yeah. Little Miss Too Polite was pissed. And she had every right, truth be told. "I was on my way to the bar to get us a couple of drinks, but as you can see, I got held up."

"I can see that." Christ, she was cute. Asher didn't miss her quick intake of breath when he took her hand, and yeah, he felt it, too—the unmistakable zing of attraction he'd felt earlier, stronger now that they were touching. He brushed his thumb over her knuckles as he raised them to his lips. Damn, she smelled good. Tropical and completely edible.

She pulled her hand away with a nervous laugh. "So, ah, yeah." She hooked a thumb toward the bar. "I'll just go grab those drinks."

Asher hoped she didn't bring him one of those fruity frozen jobs, but it would look suspicious if he told her what to order. He'd just pretended to be her boyfriend. Drink preference was the kind of thing couples knew about each other, right? He didn't know. He didn't do the couple thing. Being a SEAL wasn't conducive to a lasting relationship. His own family was proof of that.

His dad had been a SEAL, gone more days than he was home, before being killed in action when Asher was sixteen. Gracie had still been in the womb, and his mom had nearly been destroyed. If she hadn't been close to giving birth, she might've let the grief take her. Even still, she'd walked around like a zombie for the first year. Asher helped where he could, but his mom struggled to raise an infant and a teenage boy on her own. She cried a lot back then, when she thought he couldn't hear.

Asher had joined the Navy when it became obvious he

wasn't cut out for college. He worked his ass off and became a SEAL at age twenty-four. His primary objective was to ensure his mom and sister were taken care of, but where he'd followed his dad's footsteps into the Navy, he wouldn't follow them into marriage. No way he would put a woman through what his dad put his mom through. The constant disappearances. The cancelled plans. The lengthy deployments. The stress over the dangerous job, a job Asher happened to love. It was easier to remain unattached.

What he did couldn't be considered dating. If he met a woman he found attractive and if she wanted to play, he was up front about expectations before the clothes came off. Lots of orgasms. Nothing more. Well, maybe dinner, before or after the sex. He wasn't a complete jackass.

"Would you like anything special this time?" Brooke asked and Asher had the urge to kiss her. He resisted, since he was pretty sure she'd punch him.

He shook his head and glanced pointedly at the glass in Brett's hand. "You know I don't go for that girly shit. Bourbon, neat, is always gonna be my drink of choice, sweetheart." He tried to sound apologetic, as if this was a discussion they'd had before.

"Right. A real man's man, aren't you, *babe*." Then, she surprised the hell out of him by rising up on her toes and whispering a breathy "Thank you," close to his ear. Her lips caressed his cheek for the briefest of moments before she moved away.

The nearness of her mouth to any part of his body lit him up like the night sky on the Fourth of July. Made him want to get reacquainted in a down and dirty kind of way.

"Hurry back." Asher tipped his head, watching as she weaved through the tables. Once she was safely placing their orders with the bartender, he turned back to Brett, whose stupid ass was still hanging around.

Asher straightened, dwarfing the kid. He crossed his arms, knowing the pose would make his biceps bulge in all the right places. He wasn't above posturing if a guy had the size or bulk to back it up. He happened to have both.

"You wanna explain what you were doing with your hands all over my girl?"

Brett squared his shoulders. "Don't have a cow, man. We were just looking to have a little fun."

Have a cow? The kid deserved to get his ass kicked for that expression alone.

"Did she look like she was having fun to you?" Asher knew what kind of *fun* frat boy and his douchebags were looking for, and it boiled his blood.

Frat boy smirked. "We would've made it good for her."

Asher dropped the pussy with one punch.

"Unless you wanna wear your blood on the outside, I wouldn't try it," Asher cautioned the four guys at the asshole table who rose to their feet. The group varied in size, but Asher had no doubt he could take them if they were stupid enough to come at him. Keeping an eye on the group, he held a palm out to stay the now-concerned bartender and a wide-eyed Brooke. He had this. He didn't need their interference.

On the ground, Brett groaned as his friends argued in hushed tones.

They were starting to attract a crowd. A few passers-by stopped in the sand. A couple of the beachgoers craned their necks around lounge chairs to see what was going on. Asher needed to shut this shit down before his mom and sister came running. He didn't want either one of them anywhere near these bozos.

"What's the play here, boys?" Asher asked, giving them a chance to step up or step out.

"We don't want any trouble," one of them finally said, stepping forward to help Brett to his feet.

Asher addressed the whole group. "Let me be very clear. Touch my girl again..." he thought about Gracie and amended, "Touch *any* girl at this resort without permission, and you'll limp back to your mommy's and daddy's. You get me?" He eyeballed Brett. "That cabana down the beach you were bragging about? You should go there. Now."

A few curse words were mumbled as the boys hit the sand. Since there was no fucking wall to place his back against, Asher took the chair at Brooke's table that allowed him the best view of the retreating group. They were headed down the beach in the opposite direction of the hotel when Brooke returned to the table. She clunked his bourbon down hard enough to crack the mosaic table top. Seemed the glass was as stout as the rotgut, since both held steady.

Brooke slipped into the chair across from him. Her drink got a more delicate treatment. She sipped from the tall glass that had a sprig of mint on the top and then set it on a napkin. She rested her forearms against the table and laced her fingers around the glass, seemingly not inclined to talk around an elephant the size of Texas.

Tension charged the air between them, making his skin prickle with awareness and his hands eager to get reacquainted with her body. It seemed when it came to Brooke Ramsey, nothing had changed. Asher had been with his share of women, but Brooke was the only one who ever triggered his inner caveman. Triggered ideas like *mine* and *forever*. The only woman who ever tempted him to throw aside his beliefs about relationships and give one a try. So he left.

The only thing harder than walking away would've been to stay with the knowledge that one day this beautiful creature would suffer heartache, and it would be all his fault.

Asher cleared his throat. Brooke's gaze met his over the rim of the highball. What did one say to the woman he spent a month fucking nine ways to Sunday before bugging out of her life in the dead of night?

And then it hit him.

"In all the gin joints..." he started, remembering her love for the movie *Casablanca*. It was her favorite. She also loved custard-filled pastries, preferred tea over coffee, and had a kinky side that included being restrained in bed.

He grinned at that last bit. Asher earned his nickname with legitimate, work-related tasks, but his ability to tie a decent knot had started with her. Everything started with her.

He'd done the right thing, hadn't he? He'd been so sure at the time. Seeing her now, though, all golden-skinned and beautiful...

"In all the towns..." he continued, knowing the line by heart.

Brooke's laugh was the greatest sound he'd ever heard. A little light, a little grumbly, and a whole lot of sexy. It was the kind of laugh that lit up her face. The kind that made everyone within earshot smile along with her.

He could listen to that sound for the rest of his life.

Fuck.

2

BROOKE'S first thought was that her eyes were playing tricks on her.

Asher Dillon.

She'd dreamed about the man a thousand times over the years. Today wouldn't be the first time she thought she saw him in the world outside her bedroom. Not by a long shot. In fact, anytime she saw a chiseled jaw, hair the color of dark chocolate, or shoulders wide enough to strain a woman's thighs, Brooke would do a double take, thinking of him.

Once she realized the truth—that the man standing beside her with biceps for days was indeed the star of her nighttime fantasies—the anger hit, surprising her with its strength.

Eight fucking years without a single word.

Brooke met Asher in the month before she started graduate school. Asher had just finished training and was waiting to be assigned to a SEAL team. The days that followed were a blur of laughter, food, alcohol, and orgasms. So many orgasms, delivered in the most imaginative ways.

Their fling hadn't been all fun and games. Asher went to

the base to check in and hit the gym each day. She had a part-time summer internship at the company where she now worked. They never made plans for a repeat, yet each afternoon when she arrived home he was there, waiting. Sometimes with dinner. Sometimes with her favorite sweet treat from the bakery on the corner. Always thoughtful. Always hard and ready. For her. It was the happiest month of her life.

And then one morning Asher was gone. No warning. No goodbye. Just an empty space beside her in bed and sheets that continued to smell like him for months after no matter how many times she washed them.

They hadn't made commitments, but it hurt that he thought so little of her after what they shared that she didn't even warrant a kiss goodbye or a phone call to let her know he was alive. She thought, at the very least, they were friends.

Oh, he explained how his life would be once his new job started—never knowing when he'd be called out or for how long, scheduled deployments to places he couldn't talk about, yada, yada, yada. She didn't care about any of that. She didn't need a man in her back pocket 24/7. She just needed one who would treat her with the respect and trust she deserved.

That man was *not* Asher Dillon.

Who the hell did he think he was, storming back into her life all buff and bad ass, pretending to be her boyfriend as if he'd crawled out of her bed only an hour ago?

Time, it seemed, hadn't dulled the emotions Asher invoked. And boy did he invoke some doozies.

It was too much to take all at once.

The trip to the bar gave Brooke a reprieve to gather her wits. It didn't take long. She had plenty of experience.

Her life had been a study in adaption, beginning when her dad walked out. In the days that followed, Brooke's world shifted, turned upside down, inside out. Her mom turned into a wild teenager overnight, leaving Brooke to her own devices for weeks at a time. Brooke had only been nine years old, but there had been no time to wallow. Life didn't stop because things went wonky. She learned to cook and do laundry. She got herself to and from school. She did what she had to do to survive. It was a pattern she'd repeat throughout her life—circumstances shifted, she adapted.

When her mom remarried and divorced a second and third time within the first two years after her dad left—shift, adapt. On her fourteenth birthday when she learned she'd been adopted as an infant—shift, adapt. When she lost her college scholarship because her mom forgot to sign the paperwork—shift, adapt. When she woke up alone after a month filled with the best sex of her life—shift, adapt. And realizing the giver of the best sex of her life was the man who just pretended to be her boyfriend—shift, fucking adapt.

By the time she delivered Asher's bourbon and took the seat across from him, Brooke managed to wrap her head around this new reality where she and Asher were apparently staying at the same resort, he was pretending to be her boyfriend, and she was pretending the sight of him hadn't flayed her chest wide open.

"In all the world..." he continued. His voice was deeper than she remembered. Less playful despite his words, with more grit.

"Yeah, yeah," she said, unable to keep the smile from her face. "I know the line. *Casablanca* is my favorite movie."

A grin wrinkled his cheeks. "Why do you think I picked that quote?"

"You remember my favorite movie?"

Brooke's walls went up hard. She would not be charmed. After a series of failed romances, she had given up on the idea of settling down, having a family of her own. She was an independent, career-focused woman now. She had two weeks to prepare a killer advertising campaign for the Midnight Bay Beach Resort, and that's what she was going to do.

Asher pushed his sunglasses to the top of his head. His confident, honey-brown gaze bore into her. "I remember a lot of things about you, Brooke."

After the way he left, she didn't understand why he'd bother. Maybe he just had a head for trivial facts about the women he banged. Her love for Bogie packed away along-side another woman's love of 80's rock, of which, by the way, Brooke was also a fan.

It wasn't her business what he did or didn't remember. She was at the resort to work, not reminisce with an old hookup.

"What are you doing here?" The moment the question was out of her mouth, Brooke regretted asking. The resort was a tropical paradise. Obviously, he was on vacation. What if he was there with a woman? Or worse, what if he was on his *honeymoon*? Oh, man. Brooke would die of embarrassment if Asher had to explain to his new wife how he'd gotten her out of a jam.

She groaned. "Please tell me you're not on your honeymoon."

"What?" He laughed with surprised horror. "No. I'm not married."

"Here with a girlfriend?" She was intruding where she had no right, but she wouldn't take back the question. She had to know.

One of his thick brows kicked up. "Trying to ascertain if I'm single?"

"Trying to ascertain my level of humiliation."

"You don't have anything to be humiliated about, even if I did have a girlfriend. Which, for the record, I don't." His lips curled to one side. "Unless we're counting fake ones?"

Brooke shook her head to let him know they were definitely *not* counting those. Their pretend relationship ended the moment Brett and his friends left the bar.

Asher settled back in his chair. "I'm with my mom and sister. They booked the trip and I took leave to tag along."

The genuine affection in his expression melted her heart. Brooke felt her walls slip. Looking out for the people he loved was a trait she found endearing in a man, and on Asher it was sexy as hell.

"A family vacation. That's nice." Not that she'd know. The only thing she did with her mother these days was argue, and she hadn't heard from her father in years. The thought of vacationing with either one of them made her skin itch.

"More like I didn't want them leaving the United States without protection."

"Why? Grand Turks is as safe an island as they come." When he arched an incredulous brow, Brooke rolled her eyes. "Intoxicated, over-eager college boys notwithstanding."

"That dude was more than an over-eager college boy. He's a menace to women. He's lucky I pulled that punch. If the punk had messed with my sister, he wouldn't have walked away."

His words stung. Brooke didn't want the guy maimed for God's sake, but just once in her life it would be nice to have someone believe she was worth the depth of that emotion.

"Lucky for him it was just me then."

Asher's gaze narrowed. "That's not what I meant."

Brooke waved him off. She usually did a better job at hiding her insecurities. She mentally stiffened her spine and shoved those bitches back where they belonged, buried deep. A long draw from her mojito helped the process along.

"It doesn't matter. You helped me out of an awkward situation and I'm grateful. Seriously, Asher. Thank you." She raised her glass in silent toast and took another pull from the straw.

"You said you were on leave. You're still with the teams, then?" She didn't know the lingo, but Asher smirked, so she must've gotten close.

He nodded. "Still a SEAL. For the next six months, at least."

"What happens in six months?"

"My contract expires."

"You're leaving the Navy?" He'd been pumped to be a SEAL. She wondered what had happened over the years to make him want to give it up.

"Maybe." He shrugged, then scrubbed a hand over his short hair. "Christ. I dunno. Can we talk about something else?"

For the first time since their reunion Brooke saw the exhaustion hiding in the tiny wrinkles around his eyes. She'd be lying if she said she wasn't affected by him. Regardless of how they'd ended, she'd given a piece of herself to this man—a piece he still had, though he didn't know it. Seeing the weight of the world in his eyes just then made her ache to offer comfort.

She reached across the table and squeezed his hand. It wasn't much, but it was all she would allow herself to do.

"What would you like to talk about?"

He studied her for a moment before his eyes went heavy-lidded. "You're still incredibly beautiful." His thumb danced across her knuckles. "And soft."

Oh, boy. Brooke's body heated and not from the Caribbean sun. She needed to be careful around this man or she was likely to lose her head. And her panties.

She eased her hand from his. "And you're still handsome and too charming for your own good. I'm glad we got that out of the way. New topic, please."

Asher laughed, the sound rough and deep. "All right, sassy girl. Have it your way. Tell me what you're doing these days. Where do you work? Are you married? Got a boyfriend, other than me?"

His wink did funny things to her insides. Made her heart race and her stomach flutter. How sad was it that having Asher as her fake boyfriend for five minutes had been more thrilling than the entirety of her last relationship?

"I'm an advertising executive with the Woodson Bellamy Agency in San Diego."

"The place you did the summer internship?"

"Yes," she said slowly. How did he remember that? Brooke's walls slipped a little more and she grappled to hold on. "They hired me before the fall semester started that year. They let me work around my class schedule so it was a great deal." On-the-job training and the company foot the bill for her master's degree. Great didn't begin to cover it. "Once I finished graduate school, I transitioned into full time. That's why I'm here, actually. I recently signed Midnight Bay as a client and my boss thought it would be a good idea for me to come experience the resort firsthand."

Well, her boss' boss thought it would be a good idea. Her boss, Sandra Davenport, hadn't been too thrilled with the idea, but that had more to do with Sandra being a jealous bitch than anything else. Sandra constantly took credit for Brooke's work, and she had seethed over Brooke single-handedly landing the Midnight Bay account.

"Tough job," he joked.

"It has its moments, but overall I can't complain." She loved her work. She loved the challenge and creativity that came with selling products and services people didn't necessarily need but would desperately want if she did her job well.

"That answers what you do for work. What about the rest of it?"

He wanted her relationship status? Teasing him seemed appropriate, since he'd done the same to her. Brooke batted her eyelashes, enjoying the conversation more than she should. "The rest of what?"

Asher dropped his elbows onto the table and leaned toward her. His light cologne combined with the tropical air made for a heady scent. "Someone's looking to have her pretty ass spanked."

Brooke couldn't stop the gasp from leaving her mouth. He did *not* just go there.

"Asher," she warned, but the damage was done. Her body came alive, as if his words were the jumper cables to her neglected battery. All of a sudden, her skin felt too tight. A tantalizing rush of heat flooded her veins. Down below her pussy clenched, the moisture building between her legs threatening to seep through the thin lining of her swimsuit.

"God, I can't believe you said that."

He sat back and shrugged, just a guy on vacation without a care in the world. "Tell me I'm wrong."

This couldn't be happening. How pathetic was she to get all hot and bothered over a guy who'd dumped her like a bad habit? Where was her self-respect? She hadn't lived like a nun, for God's sake. She wasn't that hard up.

"You're wrong."

He smirked and she followed his glance to the front of her swimsuit. Yeah, she wasn't hiding anything. There was no mistaking the tips of her breasts straining against the fabric of the suit.

"I don't think I am." His head tilted to the side. "How long has it been since you've had a proper fuck?"

Mortification, thy name is Brooke. Her cheeks burned with it. "Pick a new topic or this conversation is over," she snapped, proud that her voice didn't waver.

God. She'd had sex, but she hadn't been properly fucked in eight years. Not that he needed to know that, the arrogant jerk.

"I wasn't kidding when I told Brett I had work to do." When Asher just stared at her, Brooke shoved her chair back intending to grab her things and go back to her suite. She had a hard enough time not using Asher as a base for comparison for all other men. He didn't have to throw it in her face that she'd found them all lacking.

"All right, all right." He showed her his palms. "You win. We'll come back to that."

She really and truly wanted to hit him. "There's nothing to come back to. My sex life is none of your business."

He didn't confirm or deny his agreement. "Relax. Would you like another drink?"

Brooke glanced down, surprised to see her glass was empty save the ice and sprigs of mint. She blew out a breath. Would she?

For eight years, she wondered what happened on the last night they spent together—why had he vanished like a thief in the night? Now was her chance to get some answers.

To get closure on the brief part of her life that colored the lens with which she viewed all men.

"Sure. Why not?"

Maybe then she could finally forget him.

3

———

ASHER WAS DRUNK, and not from the bourbon. Subtle hints of coconut and pineapple and warm, sexy woman were what made his head light. And his dick heavy.

Brooke Ramsey was a walking wet dream in that plain-Jane, sky blue swimsuit that hugged her tits in the best way. He didn't need eyes to know their perfect shape. He'd spent hours caressing, kneading, sucking those gorgeous mounds until he'd committed them to memory. And fuck him running, her nipples remembered him, too. The tight points had been reaching for him all afternoon, begging for him to play.

"I should get going."

"So soon?" Asher checked his watch, surprised to find the better part of the afternoon gone.

"We've been sitting here for several hours."

She was right. He was supposed to meet his mom and sister for dinner in less than an hour, but he didn't want this time with Brooke to end. As though years hadn't separated them, they fell into an easy banter, talking and laughing and drinking to the live soundtrack of waves lapping against the shore. For the first time in forever, Asher felt ... relaxed.

"You sure you don't have time for one more?"

"It's been really great to hang out with you again, Asher, but I do need to get some work done tonight. If I have another drink, all I'll want to do is fall into bed and sleep until morning."

Such a shame. He could think of at least ten things he'd rather do with her in bed than sleep. But, that would require an invitation.

"Where are you headed? Did the resort give you an office to work out of?" He didn't know how those things worked.

"Oh, no. I'll work out of my suite."

She didn't sound pretentious. The entire hotel was made up of suites. His was damn nice. It was bigger than his studio apartment in Coronado and was right next door to the suite his mom and sister occupied.

Brooke reached down and pulled sunglasses from a beach bag. She slid them over her eyes. The next item out of the bag was a floppy straw hat with a giant matching bow on one side. Asher couldn't keep the smile from his face when she shoved the thing on her head. She was so damn cute it killed him.

Asher checked his phone and saw a text from his mom, letting him know she and Gracie had gone back to their room to rest before dinner.

He stood and stretched his long legs. Then he walked around to her chair. He took the beach bag, tossed the strap over one shoulder, and offered her a hand.

She seemed pleased but surprised by the gesture. She slid her hand into his, and Asher steadied her as she got to her feet. Enjoying the feel of her skin against his, he laced their fingers together. With his free hand, he reached under the hat to tuck a stray hair behind her ear.

"Mind if I walk with you?" He hadn't seen Brett or any of his buddies around, but that didn't mean they weren't lurking somewhere. He'd feel better knowing she made it safely back to her room.

She looked down at their joined hands, brows pinched. "Ah, sure. I guess."

He nodded, happy to delay their parting for a few more minutes. He had roughly two more weeks at the resort. He knew she had a job to do, but he was hoping they could make plans to see each other again.

Asher pointed them in the direction of the hotel and set the pace for a slow stroll across the beach. He had carefully avoided any mention of the past, but the weight of his choices pressed down on him. He could see it in her eyes. She wanted an explanation. Hell, she deserved one. But what was he supposed to say? That he left for her own good because he had started to fall in love with her? Yeah, that would go over like a lead balloon.

Asher had wondered about her a lot over the years, but he honestly thought he'd gotten over her. The last couple of hours had proved how wrong he was. He hadn't gotten over shit, and now that she was there with him, he wanted her as much as he ever had. He wasn't sure a little fun in the sun would be enough this time, and that thought gave him pause.

How much would she be willing to give? How much would *he*? That was the real question. He had a commitment to the Navy for the next six months, at least. He wasn't sure he was ready to retire and had only just now started thinking about what might come after.

All too soon they were closing in on the elegant, open

thruway that lead to the main part of the hotel. Before they could get there, Brooke tugged on his hand.

"I'm over this way," she explained. "My suite has beach-front access."

Asher frowned, not liking the sound of that. Rooms on the ground level tended to be targets for thieves due to their easy access and multiple entry points.

She led him around a set of hedges—a perfect place for someone like frat boy Brett to lie in wait—to a wide cobble-stone walkway that was lined with more hedges and brightly colored plants and flowers.

Brooke drew in a deep breath. "Doesn't it smell amazing here?"

"Yeah, sure." Like the inside of a box of Fruity Pebbles or some shit. "You don't walk this way at night." He didn't know if he was asking or telling.

"Why wouldn't I?" She pointed to the strategically placed torches. "The path is well lit."

"By firelight? That's debatable. It's too secluded."

She bumped his arm with her shoulder. "I think it's meant to be romantic."

Asher snorted in disgust. He didn't have anything against romance, but he had a big fucking problem with Brooke being alone on this path at night. Especially after the crap that happened at the bar earlier.

"Just do me a favor and use the inside access to your suite after dark, okay?"

They turned up a short walkway that led to a small, private patio. They bypassed the oversized lounge chair and stopped in front of a huge sliding glass door. She turned to face him. "You're being silly. I'm perfectly safe here."

Maybe, but no place was completely secure. It didn't

make sense to him that she wouldn't take every precaution to keep herself out of harm's way.

"I've seen enough to know it pays to be cautious." He squeezed her fingers. "You can never be too careful. Promise me, Brooke."

"I don't know why you even—" She blew out a breath and released his hand, almost flinging him away. "Fine. Whatever. I promise."

He was used to his protective ways irritating the women in his life, so Brooke's annoyance barely registered.

"Thank you." He visually inspected the door. From what he could see it had a disengaged Charley bar off to one side and a card key reader for the lock.

"Sliders are the easiest to jimmy," he informed her. "Even with today's technology. You'd think a swanky place like this would make better security choices. Be sure to engage the security bar on the door once you're inside."

Brooke dropped her fists to her hips. "Listen up, Mr. Military SEAL Man. You are not the boss around here. I'm a grown woman. I can take care of myself."

Asher fought back a grin. "Is that right?"

She nodded once. "Been doing it forever."

And she'd done a damn fine job, from what he could see. She might not need him, but he wanted to take care of her anyway. That was the second big fucking problem he had. One that he'd figure out later. Right now he had another, more pressing issue to deal with.

"You never answered my question."

"What question?"

Asher stepped into her space, backing her against the door. He eased the hat from her head and blindly tossed it toward one of the chairs. The sunglasses went next. As she reached up to smooth her hair, he took her hand. Holding her fist against his chest he braced his other forearm against the glass, close enough to run his dangling fingers over silky strands of hair on the top of her head. The pulse in her neck beat hard enough he could see it.

"Am I going to break some poor sucker's heart when I kiss you?" He licked his lips, already tasting her.

"Would it stop you if I said yes?"

"I didn't say *if*, sweetheart."

Asher held her gaze as he lowered his head, giving her every opportunity to stop him, praying she wouldn't. His prayers were answered in a wave of lust and succulent lips. He went slow, letting the anticipation build as he caressed and nipped at her mouth. When he couldn't wait another second to taste her, he brushed his tongue against the seam of her lips, coaxing her to open. Brooke melted against him as she let him into her mouth.

More.

Asher caressed her ponytail, then wrapped the spun silk around his fist and pulled—not hard, but enough to give him the access he sought. He let go of the hand clutching at his T-shirt and wrapped his arm around her. The bare flesh of her back warmed his hand as he trailed his palm along her spine.

She arched into him, pressing her breasts against his chest, and Asher lost his fucking mind.

He hadn't intended for the kiss get out of control. He'd only meant to have a taste. Something to remind them both how good it would be. He should've known better. No woman had ever gotten to him the way Brooke had. Time and distance hadn't dulled their connection. The years left unattended had grown the heat between them to wildfire proportions. Now unleashed, it threatened to engulf everything in its path.

Brooke broke the kiss on a gasp and shoved him back. "No," she said, her voice trembling. "You are *not* going to do this to me again."

"Do what?"

"Kiss me as though I'm what you need, when we both know I'm not."

He begged to differ. He needed her with a desperation he hadn't felt in years. "After a kiss like that, how could you doubt it?"

Her eyes filled with moisture and Asher knew the past he'd been trying to avoid had just caught up with him.

"Because you left."

And there it was. Maybe that was a good thing. Better to clear the air now so they could enjoy the next two weeks.

"Brooke..." He sighed, completely unprepared for her right hook to the gut. "Hey!" She hadn't hurt him, but still.

"You're such a jerk." Brooke shook out her fist. "How could you *leave* like that?"

"Brooke, I—"

"I looked for you, you know."

"What?"

"Not like a stalker or anything. But like someone who cared about you and wanted reassurance that you were okay. Whenever I went out, I'd people watch, looking for you. You were about to start a job that would put you in dangerous situations. I didn't expect you to fall all over yourself to keep me informed as to your well-being, but a phone call to let me know you were alive wouldn't have been remiss."

He should probably have felt chastised in the face of her fiery anger, but he only got more turned-on.

"Just answer me this—did I do something? Was it me?"
What the hell?

"No. It wasn't you at all." Is that really what she thought?

It struck him dead center to think she'd gone all those years believing she was less than perfect, when in fact she'd been *everything*. His pride would *not* allow her to go on thinking she'd done something wrong.

Without a clue how to explain, Asher let the truth tumble from his mouth. "You knew my situation." They'd talked about it more than once. "I got called up. I don't remember the exact time, but it was early. Before sunrise. You were still asleep."

Over the years he'd convinced himself he remembered that morning so well because it was the day he got assigned to his team and not because it was the day he lost her.

"I was instructed to report immediately. It was time for me to focus on my job. Believe it or not, it was hard as hell to leave you, but I had to go. My commitment was to the Navy. I was always up front about that. I didn't call or keep in contact because I thought it would be easier that way. I didn't want to hurt you."

"You can't be serious."

"I'm deadly serious." Asher gripped her shoulders. He'd never tried to verbalize how he felt before, so he wasn't sure where to start. He just knew he had to make her understand. "Being a SEAL is the best job in the world, but it's also demanding, and not just on me. My job would affect anyone I was with, too. My dad was a SEAL, so I know what it's like to be on the other side of things. I was, I *am*, proud of my dad's service, but it still sucked not having him be a part of our daily lives.

"My mom had a tough time of it, before and after my dad died in combat. They fought a lot when he was home, which wasn't often. And after, when they couldn't fight anymore..." Yeah. He couldn't go there. "It's a hard life,

Brooke, and I decided a long time ago that I wouldn't put any woman through that."

"So, that's it? You put your life on hold while you're in the military?"

"The military *is* my life."

"By default, because apparently you've shut out any other possibilities."

"There are no other possibilities." Not for him. Not while he was still active. A lot of guys with the teams felt the same way.

She shrugged him off. "That's the stupidest thing I've ever heard."

His rising anger had nothing to do with the growing probability that she was right and everything to do with the aching erection he had less and less hope of using with her.

"Do you know how high the divorce rate is for guys like me?" he snapped. "If that's not a reason to shy away from a relationship, I don't know what is."

"If that's true, those guys are either assholes or they aren't marrying the right women."

Asher thought about his SEAL brothers—Chase, Carson, and Clay—who'd recently paired up with the loves of their lives. His brothers weren't assholes, not to their ladies anyway. The love and devotion they had for their women was the real deal.

And they have all retired. Not the same situation.

"Maybe you're right, but that doesn't change anything. My life belongs to the Navy for the foreseeable future and that's just the way it is. That's how it's always been."

She nodded. "So, that kiss just now was your way of telling me you want back into my bed, but not into my life?"

The sadness in those gorgeous blues sucker punched him in the chest. Asher frowned hard. He hadn't been able to think past the consuming hunger to get inside her. He needed a second to process, which was impossible to do while she was so close.

He was in over his head here. Seeing her again had thrown him off his game. Too many things were up in the air right now. Most of his teammates were getting out. His contract was about up. His future was a huge fucking question mark. He was in no position to make any promises, but damn, he couldn't stand the thought of never seeing her again.

The *beep* and *whir* of the door lock disengaging got his attention.

"Wait. Where are you going? We're not done here."

Brooke jerked the slider open. "Yes, we are. It was great to see you, but I'm not here to hook up, Ash. I have work to do."

No one called him Ash except his mom and sister. He liked the intimacy of the name coming from her lips.

"Who says we have to hook up? We're on an island. There are other things we could do. Eat, drink, scuba dive." *Scuba dive?* Clearly the blood thickening his dick had left his brain deprived.

"I'm not certified to scuba dive."

"Snorkeling, then."

Brooke rolled her eyes. "Good night, Ash."

Not good*bye.*

"I'll take that as a yes," he told her as she slid the door closed. They weren't done. Not by a long shot.

Asher waited, holding her stare through the glass. When it became apparent she wasn't going to secure the door, he jabbed a finger toward the security bar.

"What did I tell you about that?"

With a smile he didn't trust, she stretched out her arm and deliberately dropped the bar into place.

"I'll see you tomorrow," he growled, following the path of the curtains as they flew across, effectively shutting him out.

"Go away, Asher."

He could hear the smile in her voice, and it gave him hope. It took every bit of his willpower to turn and leave, but he knew when the time came to retreat and regroup.

Asher followed the path to the hotel lobby. He got on the first available elevator and punched the button for the eighth floor.

Brooke said she didn't want to hook up, but damn. He hadn't imagined the strength in that kiss. Her tight little body arching and rubbing over him, practically begging him to fuck...

Asher groaned and banged his forehead against the wall of the empty elevator.

He needed to get his shit straight or these were going to be the longest two weeks of his life.

4

Bang, bang, bang, bang!

Asher surged up from the mattress, disoriented and tangled in the sheets. His head protested from the bottle of bourbon he'd tried to drown in the night before, and he grabbed his skull before it could split down the middle.

Bang, bang, bang, bang!

Groaning, he rolled from the bed. Once he was sure he wouldn't topple over, he bent to grab the cargo shorts he had on the day before and then pulled them over his hips. He didn't bother trying to find a shirt.

Rubbing the sleep from his eyes he stumbled out of the bedroom into the spacious living area of the suite.

Bang, bang, bang, bang!

"What the everlasting fuck?" he growled, then louder, "I'm coming. Jesus. Pipe down!"

"Ash!" Gracie yelled, pounding one more time. "Open up!"

Asher grabbed the handle and flung the door open so hard his sister took a step back.

"Whoa. Hey. You look like shit."

"Gee, thanks. What d'ya want, squirt?" Asher didn't wait for her to answer. He spun on his heel, leaving her to either catch the self-propelled door or have it slammed in her face. At this point, he didn't care which option she chose. He needed coffee, pronto. And an aspirin. Maybe two.

"Damn. What the hell is your problem?"

Asher rummaged around the wet bar, filling the pitifully small coffee maker with a ready made pod and water, then set it to brew.

"I was trying to sleep."

He turned to find Gracie eyeballing him like he was a science experiment. He tapped a finger against the Navy SEAL Trident tattoo on his left pec. "And I'm the only sailor in this family. Watch your mouth."

"Aye, aye, Captain." She gave him a hearty salute that made him laugh, the little imp. He ruffled her hair. It was the same as his, thick and dark brown. His was standard issue military cut—longer on the top than the back and sides, but Gracie's was like the girl herself, unruly, carefree, and wild.

Their mom had her work cut out for her.

Asher took the finished brew to the couch. He sat down and propped his feet on the coffee table, crossing them at the ankles. "What are you doing here, squirt? Shouldn't you be down on the beach?"

It occurred to him that he had no idea what time it was.

Gracie threw open the drapes, about blinding him, so he dropped his head to the back of the couch and closed his eyes. He heard her open the doors that led to the balcony and the humid, ocean breeze drifted into the room.

"Nah. Why would I go where all the hot dudes are when I can spend time with my grumpy-ass brother?"

Asher arched a brow without opening his eyes. "Looks

like I'm gonna have to talk to mom about your language. And about dude gawking." He raised his head to sip the coffee, letting the warmth of the brew soothe his scratchy throat.

"I'm sixteen, Ash. I'm allowed to gawk if I want."

He squinted at her tight tank top and shorts that showed off too much of her legs. Jesus, when had his baby sister gotten all grown up? She didn't look sixteen. She looked significantly older, which made him think about Brett and his band of assholes.

"Looking is one thing, but don't you ever let a guy pressure you into doing something you're not ready to do. You understand? And while we're here, you need to stay either with mom or with me. You're not to go off by yourself."

Gracie dropped her hands on her hips, reminding him of the way Brooke squared off with him the night before.

"Whatever, *Dad*. I'm not a naive little girl, you know. And I'm not stupid."

He ignored her tone, because really, did she have another one?

"Glad to hear it," he said. "Because—fair warning—I'll break the fingers of any guy who touches you." And then he'd move on to his face and legs.

Gracie jumped onto the couch like a gazelle, almost making him spill his coffee. She tucked her skinny legs underneath her and poked him in the arm.

"That one doesn't look so bad. What happened?"

Asher glanced down at the jagged red mark on the front side of his shoulder. He'd finished up a three-month deployment right before this little trip, the details of which he would never share with his little sister.

"Feral alley cat." Feline claws, six-inch Cambodian

tactical knife. Tomato, tomahto. He grinned when she rolled her eyes. "Just got the stitches out last week."

"How many?"

"Fifteen."

His sister got quiet. When she glanced up at him she had tears in her eyes. "You're okay, though, right, Ash?"

Asher cursed and set his coffee on the table. This, *this* is what he'd been trying to explain to Brooke last night. It was hard enough knowing his mom and his sister worried about him.

"C'mere, squirt." He wrapped an arm around her and pulled Gracie against his side. Just like when she was little, she dropped her head onto his shoulder. She glanced up at him, her big doe eyes looking for reassurance.

"I'm fine," he insisted. "It's just a little scratch. Nothing to worry about."

"What about in here?" She pressed a finger against his temple hard enough to tilt his head.

"What do you mean?" *Christ.* "Have you been on the internet reading about PTSD?"

"Post-traumatic stress is nothing to be ashamed about. It's a real thing."

He sat her up and turned to face her. "It is a real thing. You're absolutely right." He lifted her chin with his knuckle, forcing her to meet his gaze. "But, I don't have it. It's just a scratch, Gracie. I'm fine, really."

"Are you sure? You seemed kinda off when I first got here. Your eyes are all red and you're grumpier than usual."

"Well, if you must know, I was up half the night—"

"Inability to sleep is one of—"

"Stop it, Grace," he snapped, but damn, she wasn't doing his head any favors. He only called her Grace when his patience reached its limit, and she wisely clamped her mouth shut. "I'm only gonna say this once, so listen up. I sleep fine. I don't have nightmares. I don't get anxious. Yeah, I know the symptoms. I'm a SEAL. I know plenty of guys who struggle, but I'm not one of them. And if sometime down the road I start to have trouble, I give you my word I will deal with it. Okay?"

When Gracie bit her lip and nodded, Asher sank back into the couch and closed his eyes again, wishing he had a painkiller within reach. "And stay off the fucking internet."

"I'm six*teen*."

Asher hummed. Right. Keeping her off the internet would be equivalent to taking away her cell phone. Not happening.

"You missed dinner last night and you didn't answer any of your texts. Mom's not happy."

Asher sighed and sat up. He wasn't going to get any more rest as long as Gracie was there, so he might as well give it up. He grabbed the cup and drained what was left of the coffee down his throat.

"I'll talk to her."

Gracie followed him to the coffee maker. "We decided that we're going to grab some lunch at Seafare and then take the boat tour around the islands. Doesn't that sound like fun?" Gracie bounced on her toes. "Wanna go with us?"

No, he did not. He wanted to sleep off his hangover, and then he had a snorkeling trip to plan.

"Come on, Ash. Please?" Gracie begged. "Mom said we had to be down at the restaurant in thirty minutes."

Snorkeling. A boat tour around the islands. What was happening to him?

He grabbed the freshly brewed cup and headed toward the shower.

"I'll meet you there in twenty."

"Ms. RAMSEY, welcome to Midnight Bay Beach Resort. I hope the accommodations are to your liking." Gregory Meeks, part-owner and general manager of the resort, said with a charming smile and polite handshake.

Gregory's formal British accent and expensive tailored suit seemed out of place in the land of white sandy beaches. Brooke glanced down at her floral-patterned sundress, worried she might be underdressed.

She did a mental shrug. Nothing she could do about her outfit now, and anyway, she loved the dress. It accentuated her breasts without being gaudy or inappropriate, and the skirt fluttered around her knees like a gentle breeze. She felt pretty and vibrant and ready to dazzle the man with her creative prowess.

"My suite is perfect, Mr. Meeks. Thank you." Although there was a certain muscle-bound Neanderthal who had some issues—and not just with her suite.

She didn't know what Asher was up to with his demand to see her that day, but she'd have to stay on her toes or she might lose her heart to him again. She couldn't let that happen.

"Please, call me Gregory."

"Only if you call me Brooke."

Gregory bowed his head in consent. "I thought we could talk over lunch. Seafare is one of our outdoor restaurants." He started walking and Brooke fell in step next to him. "It's a favorite among the guests. The menu is a reflection of the rich flavors found in the Caribbean, the seafood found in its waters, and the New England flair of Chef Jonas Rancourt."

"I've heard excellent things about Chef Rancourt from my colleagues in San Diego. He ran a restaurant there for years after leaving Boston." Brooke wasn't much of a foodie, but she was excited to eat the local food made by a renowned chef.

"You shall not be disappointed."

They walked out of the hotel and took a wooden-planked path to the left. They followed the path to a sandy ridge that housed the restaurant and overlooked the ocean and beach below. The view was stunning.

Seafare was a quaint little restaurant. The floor was nothing more than sandy beach. There were no walls, allowing the warm ocean breeze to blow through. Wooden pillars wrapped in thick, marine-style ropes were placed throughout, holding up the large canopy overhead. High-gloss wooden picnic tables were placed at various intervals in the sand. Not all of the tables were the same size. There were a few two seaters mixed in with the tables that sat four, six, and even one off to the side that had seating for eight. And from her vantage point the restaurant appeared to be crowded.

Taken by the quiet charm of the space, Brooke wasn't paying attention to where she was going and her foot slipped from the edge of the walkway.

"Oh!" Gregory grabbed her elbow to steady her and somehow Brooke ended up flat against the man's chest. "Oh," She jerked back with a nervous laugh. Before she could stop herself, she smoothed the wrinkles from his lapel where she'd clutched him. "I'm so sorry."

Gregory still cupped her elbow. "Are you all right? Did you twist your ankle?"

She readjusted the bag on her shoulder and stepped back, testing her weight on it. She wasn't even wearing heels, just a cute pair of flat sandals with straps that wrapped around her ankles. "No. I think it's okay. Thank you."

Gregory offered her his elbow. "Might I offer some assistance?"

"Oh God." Brooke laughed again, feeling her cheeks heat. "I'm so embarrassed." But not stupid. When a handsome British man in a tailored suit offered his arm, a girl took it.

"Don't be silly. Happens to me all the time."

"Right. You do seem like the clumsy type," she teased, glad he didn't seem to be a stuffy, rigid type of client. Under different circumstances she might even enjoy flirting with the man.

Gregory shot her a wink. "Shall we sit?"

"Please."

Gregory led her to a table. He waited while she slid onto the bench and got herself situated before removing his jacket and taking the seat across from her. He reached for his tie.

"You don't mind, do you?" he asked as he slid the tie off. He made quick work of the top few buttons on his shirt and then rolled up the sleeves. "I don't normally dress so formally here, but I had a meeting this morning."

Gregory had nice forearms, but Brooke had seen better. Last night, in fact. Attached to a big, handsome, bossy SEAL.

"I admit I was surprised to see you in a suit."

"What did you expect? More beach bum, less British butler?"

Brooke snickered as she dug into her bag. "Something like that." She pulled out a notebook and pen and set them on the table beside her. She glanced up and froze. As though she'd conjured him with her forearm musings,

Asher was there, sitting two tables behind Gregory, facing her.

Ash's gaze locked on hers, his expression unreadable. A young girl sat beside him. Same eyes, same hair color. The resemblance was too great for her not to be his sister. That meant the woman at the table with her back to Brooke had to be Ash's mom.

A funny feeling tickled her stomach at seeing them together, as a family. It should have warmed her heart, but instead, a shock of loneliness stabbed her chest. She'd never had that, not even when her dad had been around.

Brooke had her mom, but they never spent time together. When they did, it always ended the same—with her mom finding fault with everything she did and a reminder that she should be grateful her parents had 'rescued her,' as if she were a puppy dumped at the local shelter instead of the product of an unwanted teen pregnancy. Oh yeah, she'd heard that story a few times, too.

Brooke sighed, and for a moment she let herself wonder what it would be like to sit there with them. To talk about girl things with his sister or critique the food with his mom. To be a part of something real.

It doesn't matter. He's doesn't want you to be his girlfriend, remember? He only wants in your panties, and hookups don't meet family.

Beside him the girl chatted happily, using her hands to express whatever it was she was talking about. Ash nodded a couple of times, but his gaze never left hers.

Brooke's nerves went into overdrive. His stare was potent and all-consuming, making her feel naked and exposed.

"Brooke?"

She started, Gregory's voice breaking whatever spell she'd been under. She blinked and refocused on the man in front of her. Her *client*. She would not allow Asher-freaking-Dillon to distract her from the biggest opportunity of her career.

"I'm sorry." She smiled apologetically. "I got distracted by the gorgeous view." Gregory would assume she meant the ocean view, which was also spectacular. "What were you saying?"

"I asked if you'd like to try some of the wine." He held out a wine list. "We have an excellent selection to choose from."

Brooke rejected the wine list for fear the nerves at seeing Asher would make it tremble in her hands. "Would you mind choosing? I don't know anything about wine except how to drink it."

Gregory tilted his head and laughed. "You're absolutely delightful. And thank you, I'd be happy to choose. Do you prefer red or white?"

"White, please." She remembered reading somewhere that white went better with fish.

Gregory placed their drink order and Brooke forced herself to not look over the man's shoulder at Asher. She could feel his gaze burning into her, could feel the tension from two tables away.

What did he have to be tense about? Did he think she planned to crash his little family outing? That she'd embarrass him by walking over there and making introductions? Well, he could just get over himself. She was there to work.

The waiter stopped by their table. Once their food orders were placed and the wine had been served, Brooke opened her notebook and picked up the pen, ready to get started.

"Tell me your thoughts for the new advertising campaign."

Gregory folded his hands on top of the table. "As I'm sure you know, Midnight Bay Beach Resort has six properties across the globe. Turks and Caicos will be the flagship resort for the campaign, but I'll let you in on a little secret. If we're happy with what you come up with, you will get the business for the others."

Brooke tried to keep her expression even, but inside her chest her heart rate took off like a shot. The resort was a bigger opportunity that she'd originally thought. If she could nail this campaign, the higher ups would take note and Sandra wouldn't be able to take credit. It would be all her.

Gregory kept the conversation flowing. He told her the history of the resort, explained that their local sales and marketing team would only implement her ideas, not take part in the creation process, and filled her in on their expansion project. She asked questions here and there, and by the time she'd finished her amazing lobster with jerk-rum butter, Brooke had filled half her notebook and was buzzing with excitement.

"My compliments to the chef. The lobster was delicious." She wiped her mouth with a napkin and set her plate aside. She wrote down a few notes about the flavors before the essence faded, then got to the heart of the meeting. "Corporate mentioned there might be a specific market you'd like to target with the new campaign, but they didn't give me any details."

As if on autopilot, her gaze drifted over Gregory's shoulder. She was surprised to find Asher and his family gone. She'd been so focused on work, she hadn't even seen them leave.

"That is correct. We have a large clientele of families at this location, but the new expansion that opens next year will be couple-oriented. The suites will be designed and furnished with romance in mind. There will be a private beach, along with a daily bottle of champagne and tray of strawberries. It will be quite lovely."

"That sounds wonderful." Brooke scribbled in her notebook. "And the activities? Will those be couple-centric as well?"

Gregory gave her a sly smile. "Much the same as they are now, only without children. The couples' section of the resort will have access to the primary resort, but those who stay on this property will not be allowed access into the couple-only areas, such as the pool and private beach."

Gregory studied her over his steepled hands as Brooke took a sip of the crisp chardonnay. Like the meal, it was also delicious. She jotted down information from the bottle's label so she could order it another time.

"Dare I say it was a brilliant stroke of luck that you brought your boyfriend along with you. Now you'll be able to experience the activities and the resort as a couple, which will give you the right inspiration to create the new campaign. You showed great foresight, Brooke. I like that."

Brooke choked on her wine. "I-I'm sorry? W-what?"

"Ah, right. Sorry. You're probably wondering how I know about him." He nodded, as if he could possibly understand her confusion ... since she didn't *have* a *him*.

"Whenever there's an issue on resort property, an incident report must be filed by the employee who either is involved or is witness to the event. I received a report on the situation at Cavalier's yesterday. The bartender indicated you were harassed by another guest, but that no intervention was necessary on his part since your boyfriend handled the situation. Quite expeditiously, too, from what I read."

Brooke groaned inwardly.

Shit. Shit shit *shit*.

Don't panic. They hired your company without knowing if you did or didn't have a boyfriend.

Right. She could salvage this. All she had to do was come clean about the misunderstanding. He might be disappointed that she wouldn't be able to experience the resort as one half of a couple, but she was damn good at her job. She would still deliver a kickass campaign for them, regardless.

"And since I brought it up, I'd like to apologize on behalf of the resort. The guest who bothered you has been warned and every employee on site has been informed to keep a sharp eye on the man." Gregory reached over and put his hand over hers. "Is something wrong?"

Brooke swallowed hard. Sandra would *fry* her if she heard about the incident at the bar. She'd find a way to make it Brooke's fault, she just knew it. Not to mention Sandra's nosy ass knew Brooke was single and had been for months.

"Gregory. That situation about my boyfriend, it's not—"

"Did I hear someone talking about me?" A deep, rumbling voice fingered its way down her spine.

No. This could *not* be happening.

She twirled around to find Asher behind her. He was wearing a United States Navy polo shirt, black cargo shorts, and canvas deck shoes.

Gregory slid from the bench seat and reached out his hand. "You must be the boyfriend?"

Asher cocked an arrogant brow at her before turning back to Gregory. "Asher Dillon," he said and shook Gregory's hand. "And you are?"

"Gregory Meeks. I run the resort. I heard about the situation yesterday. Thank you for your assistance."

Asher appeared to be sizing Gregory up. "I appreciate that, man, but I don't need thanks for taking care of my girl."

"No, no. Of course not." Gregory cleared his throat, obviously uncomfortable.

What was he doing? She was going to *kill* Asher if he messed this up for her.

"Ash, honey," she said through her teeth, adding as much saccharine as she could manage. "Gregory and I have been working on the new advertising campaign for the resort. We still have some work to do. Can I catch up with you later?"

"No need," Gregory said. "We've covered the basics. Now it's time for you to get out there and experience the resort. Of course, if you have any questions, you know how to reach me. Otherwise, we can touch base at the end of the week."

Gregory turned to Asher. "Do you have a plan laid out for today? I'd be happy to offer some suggestions."

"I was thinking about taking the boat tour around the islands."

"Oh, you must! It's a beautiful tour with several stops that are known to be quite romantic."

Asher grinned like a Cheshire cat. "What'd'ya say, sweetheart? Wanna go for a ride?"

Brooke was definitely going to kill him.

5

"Don't say a word," Brooke gritted out. "Not one word."

She stormed past him, following the path the manager had taken a few moments before. Asher's legs were long enough he didn't have to hurry to catch up.

"Nice dress," he couldn't help telling her, despite the warning. She looked amazing. She wore very little makeup, if any; her hair flowed down her back, held out of her face by a wide black band. There was plenty of tanned skin showing, but not so much that he'd want to gouge out the eyes of any man who looked her way.

The jealousy thing was new. It dropped over him like a bucket of ice water when he saw her in the arms of that fucking Brit. The guy had practically mauled her outside the restaurant, then stripped off half his clothes at the table. The possibility that the guy was her work contact was the only thing that kept Asher in his seat.

Brooke stopped in her tracks and huffed. Holy hell, he wanted to know what that pique tasted like. Wanted it on his tongue, down his throat.

"Not funny."

"What? You said one word. That was two."

Yeah, his little firecracker wasn't having any of that. She started off again, angrily stomping through the sand. Asher cursed. He didn't feel like chasing her halfway down the crowded beach, and he was running out of time. The boat tour started in twenty minutes.

Why the fuck he decided Brooke should join in the family outing, Asher didn't know. Having her there would definitely complicate things, but he was running on instinct at this point. Everything inside him demanded he go back to the restaurant and get her, so that's what he'd done. He hadn't thought much past that point.

He spied an empty cabana. Perfect. Asher snaked an arm around Brooke's waist, lifting her off the ground, pressing her back against his chest. She gritted out his name and tried to kick him as he marched the fifty or so feet to the place that would separate them from watchful eyes. Once inside, Asher set her on her feet and yanked the tied-back fabric loose, closing them in.

First things first.

Asher swooped down and pressed his mouth to hers. Using her surprise to his advantage, he dipped into her mouth and groaned. She tasted like his favorite brand of bourbon. A little sweet. A little spicy. Every ounce going to his head.

He couldn't get enough.

He hauled her against his chest and then she was right there with him, her tongue pressing over his to gain access to his mouth. He wanted nothing more than to let her play, but his family was waiting.

He broke the kiss, nipping her bottom lip then soothing the sting with a soft lick. He loosened his arms, letting her slide down his body until her feet were firmly on the sand.

He rested his forehead against hers and tried to catch his breath. "Always so good with you, sweetheart."

"I told you," she said, breathless. "I'm not here to hook up."

"You and I have very different definitions for what that means. Trust me when I say what we just did doesn't even come close to mine."

He kissed her forehead and stepped back. "Are you ready to talk about what started that fire under your ass?"

She didn't waste any time laying into him.

"Do you have any idea what could happen if the resort found out we lied to them? Or, God, my agency? My boss is a real bitch, Ash. She's been gunning for me for years. She wouldn't think twice about using this against me to either steal the account or get me fired for unprofessional conduct. And if I try to come clean now, I'll look like an idiot to the client. Not to mention the trust I'd lose with the client and my company." She was pacing now. "This is not how I do business. I feel like you've put me in an impossible situation."

"First of all, no one lied."

"You said you were my boyfriend!"

"No, I *insinuated* I was your boyfriend. Not the same thing."

"I still don't know why you'd—"

"Hear me out." He needed to talk fast. "We didn't lie. That Gregory guy made an assumption and we didn't correct him. It's not the end of the world. I guarantee they don't give a shit one way or the other, as long as you give them a kickass campaign. And from what I heard, Gregory liked the idea of us doing things together on the island, so why not? Our private business is just that. Not the resort's. Not your agency's. *Ours*."

"Ash, I—"

"I'm not finished." Damn, he wished he had time to think this shit through, but the clock was ticking. He wasn't ready to let Brooke go just yet, and if he missed the tour boat, his mom and sister would murder him. Besides, he'd given his word that he'd be there, and he never went back on his word. Sink or swim time.

"Your boss isn't here, so there's no need to worry about her. And besides, didn't you say you landed this account on your own? If your boss is such a bitch, maybe you should consider taking the resort's business and doing your own thing."

"I can't just..." Brooke burst out laughing, easing the tension in his shoulders. "It's not that simple."

Asher smiled and couldn't resist pulling her into a hug. "I know it's not, sweetheart. But, listen, I promise we can talk this to death later if you want, but right now I've got some-place to be and I want you to come with me. Can it be enough for now that I want to spend time with you?" Damn near begging now, he added, "Just give me today, and we can figure out the rest later. Can you do that?"

It felt like a year before she gave a soft consent.

"Good." He exhaled and, because he could, caressed his thumb over the contour of her cheek. God, she was soft. "Now, take off your sandals."

"What? Why?"

Asher kicked off his own shoes and hooked them with his fingers. "Come on, come on. You heard me, sassy girl. Take off those sandals."

Realizing he was serious, Brooke bent down and worked the straps on her shoes.

He checked his watch and cursed.

"Now what?" she asked as she shoved the shoes into her bag and dug her toes into the warm sand.

He took her hand and tugged her out of the cabana.

"Now we run."

BROOKE WAS WINDED by the time they hit the dock. Ash didn't give her time to collect her bearings before he jumped onto the back platform of a waiting catamaran. Since their hands were still linked, Brooke had no choice but to leap with him. He turned in time to catch her. She gripped his biceps as their chests collided, his hard and unforgiving enough against her breasts to draw a quiet *oomph* from her throat.

Asher's arms tightened around her middle. The husky laugh close to her ear went straight to her girly parts. Goosebumps branched out, leaving no part of her skin unaffected.

Exhilarated from the mad dash down the beach as much as the man, Brooke gave in to the sensation. She wrapped her arms around his neck, threw her head back, and laughed with him as he spun her aboard.

"Where are you taking me, crazy man?"

Ash nuzzled her neck, the scruff that hadn't been there yesterday making her nerves tingle.

"You're beautiful," he whispered against her ear. "Don't be mad."

He kissed her hard, then released her so fast Brooke had to grab onto the railing to keep from losing her balance and falling overboard.

"Where have you been?" A shrill voice demanded from above them. "We almost left without you!"

Together, Brooke and Ash looked skyward. Brooke's

elation suffered a swift death as she recognized the young girl on the upper deck as the one who was with Ash at the restaurant.

Oh no. What was he *doing*?

"Quit being dramatic, squirt. I said I'd be here. I'm here. Where's Mom?"

"Had to run back to the room for something. She'll be right back."

"So you weren't waiting on me after all."

The girl shrugged. "I see you've made a friend." Her smile seemed forced, sarcastic even, when she glanced at Brooke. "Hi."

"Hi." A swarm of butterflies took flight in Brooke's stomach. Her heart joined in the flurry, making it hard to draw a decent breath. Of all the things she imagined he would plan for them, a boat trip with his family was not anywhere on her radar. Brooke could keep him at arm's length as long as they kept this thing, whatever it was, casual and fun.

This was not what she signed up for.

She agreed—against her better judgment and because she never had been able to resist him—to give him a day. Twenty-four hours to spoil herself with the sexy, bossy man who pushed all her buttons. She could keep her heart safe for one day while they re-explored their chemistry, and took in the island. But, *this*. A family outing? If she had to spend the day watching them together, feeling the love and connection she'd seen at the restaurant earlier while she stood firmly on the outside ... she wasn't sure she could do it.

She'd loved Asher once. She was afraid she could fall again. Her rational brain knew he wasn't trying to hurt her, but the lonely girl inside her that craved love and affection thought it was cruel of Asher to flaunt what he'd clearly told her they could never have together. A future.

She had to get off the boat and back on solid ground.

"I'm Grace, Asher's sister." The girl's gaze narrowed and Brooke almost laughed. She looked so much like her brother just then, fierce and protective, making Brooke's heart ache a little more. "Who're you?"

"Don't be rude, Gracie. This is Brooke Ramsey, a friend of mine from way back. She's here on business and we ran into each other yesterday. We haven't seen each other for a while, so I invited her to come along with us today."

"Of course you did." Disappointment tugged at Grace's pretty features. "And why wouldn't you? It's not like we're required to spend any time together or anything."

Ash slid an arm around Brooke's waist and pulled her in close. It was a possessive move. One Brooke didn't understand. "We're going to spend the entire day together, Gracie. All of us. It'll be fun."

Fun wasn't the word Brooke would've chosen.

"Whatever." Grace turned and dropped onto the bench facing the canopy-covered area where the captain sat preparing to get them underway. Grace leaned back and draped her arms over the railing behind her.

"Grace." The reprimand in Ash's tone was clear, but the girl ignored him.

Brooke stifled a groan. Damn it all. Why? Why would he put her in this awkward situation?

He said they didn't have to hook up in order to hang out. He also said a relationship wasn't in the cards for him. So, what exactly did he want from her? Were they going to be *friends* now?

Brooke didn't know how she felt about that. The man had been inside her body, repeatedly and at length. She knew the sound he made when he came, the way his body and mouth moved on hers. Could she be friends with a man she'd spent the last eight years craving like a junkie fresh out of rehab?

Everything about this situation, about Ash, confused her and she didn't like it.

You don't have time to be confused. You have a job to do.

"Ash, it's okay." In all honesty, Brooke couldn't blame his sister for being upset. Grace hadn't expected to have to share her brother with anyone. Why would she? They were on a family vacation, and Brooke wasn't—and would never be —family.

Brooke tried to pry her hand loose from Asher's, but he held tight.

"You should spend time with your family," she said. "I need to get to work anyway. We can catch up later."

"No, it's not okay and you aren't going anywhere." He pressed a gentle kiss against her temple and lowered his voice so only she could hear. "I want you here. Don't worry about Gracie. She's sixteen." He tilted his face toward where Grace sat and Brooke would swear she saw his eyes slit behind his Oakley's. "She's not a bad girl, but it seems she developed an attitude during my last deployment. And the mouth to go with it."

"It's not unreasonable that she would want to spend time with you. I can't blame her for wanting you all to herself."

His shadow fell across her face, shielding her from the bright sunshine. He slid his sunglasses to the top of his head. His eyes were rich pools of caramelized sin. He stroked a finger down the side of her neck. "Is that what *you* want? To have me all to yourself?"

Brooke couldn't help it. Her gaze dropped to his mouth

as her body remembered the kiss from the night before. "No, of course not. That would be against rule number one."

"There's a rule?" His hand slipped around to cup the back of her neck. A gentle squeeze at the base of her skull brought her to the balls of her feet, inching her close enough to his mouth to feel his breath against her lips.

"W-we talked about this." The gentle sway of the boat rocked her into him. Their chests bumped and Ash tightened his grip, holding her flush against his body. Their hips brushed in a way that felt wicked in public. Brooke bit her bottom lip to stifle the groan when she felt him begin to harden.

"Did we?"

"Yes," she said, wishing the word had come out stronger than a breath. "No sex. Remember?" Down below, her body denied the declaration with a quick clench and she had to remind herself why it wouldn't be a good idea to climb on and grind him hard.

"Having me all to yourself doesn't have to end with sex, sweetheart." His lips brushed hers, light as a feather. "There are so many other things we could do. Or have you forgotten?"

Brooke closed her eyes, fighting against the images threatening to turn her into a horny slut right there in front of God and Grace.

She hadn't forgotten one moment of their time together. She'd had boyfriends, lovers, since Ash, but none of them had mastered her body as he had.

"I don't mean to interrupt," a voice called out. "But can an old woman get some help aboard?"

Brooke jumped back, breaking the contact. Oh God. He'd done it to her *again*. What was it about this man that made her forget ... everything?

Brooke's face flamed hot as she took in the woman standing on the dock with her hand outstretched. Old, her ass. The woman who had to be Asher's mom was tiny in stature, but not in presence. She was tanned and fit, confident in the sheer cover-up that barely shielded the sparkling green two-piece underneath. She had a kind smile and warm hazel eyes. A slight graying at her temples was the only betrayal of the youthful looking woman's age.

Asher took her hand and offered support as she hopped on deck with ease.

"Thanks, kiddo."

A giggle slipped from Brooke's throat. Only a mother could get away with calling a six-three behemoth of a man such as Asher "kiddo."

Asher's lips twitched. "Mom, this is my friend Brooke. She's going to join us today."

Oh, no, she's not.

Without his hands and mouth and sexy reminders to distract her, Brooke's survival instincts surged to the surface. She couldn't spend the day getting to know his mom and sister when she didn't even know where she stood with Asher. She couldn't get attached, to any of them.

"Hello, Brooke. It's nice to meet you. I'm Ellen."

"It's nice to meet you as well."

"Now that everyone is on board, let's roll," the captain called down.

The engine roared and Brooke's time ran out. She darted a glance over her shoulder to gauge the distance to the dock. The boat slowly edged forward. She could make it if she moved, now. "I'm sorry, Ellen. I wish I could stay, but Ash seems to have forgotten I have work to do. I do hope you enjoy your trip around the islands, though."

Ellen's brow lifted in curiosity as Asher's slammed down.

"What do you mean? Hey!" Ash yelled as she launched off the back of the boat, her feet barely making purchase with the edge of the dock. "Brooke!"

She had a moment of panic, arms flailing, before she leaned forward and was able to right herself.

"Damn it, what're you trying to do? Kill yourself?" Asher growled from the boat behind her.

Brooke took a second to compose herself. She adjusted the bag on her shoulder and turned to face the retreating boat. Ash stood strong on the platform, arms crossed, his body in perfect sync with the machine as it picked up speed.

She knew full well he could make the captain stop or turn around at any moment, or, God forbid, jump ship and come for her. She wasn't going to risk creating an even bigger scene. Ignoring the loneliness that settled in her chest, Brooke waved, blew him a kiss, then turned to run up the dock toward the beach.

"Now you owe me," he called after her. "And you can bet I'll be coming to collect."

6

ASHER WAS in a strange mood when he walked into Sundowner, Midnight Bay's premier restaurant located on the roof of the main hotel. He was a decisive man who knew his own mind. He wasn't used to feeling at odds, and it seemed the whole day had conspired to throw him off his game.

For starters and much to his surprise, he actually enjoyed the day on the water. He swam for the hell of it. Combed a secluded beach looking for shells with Gracie. Lazed in the sun while tossing back an ice-cold beer with his mom. For a while there, he was reminded of a time before he became a SEAL, when the ocean wasn't something that tried to kick his ass every time his feet cracked the surface. When the hot sand wasn't something that dug into every available crevice and *stayed there*.

As fun and relaxing as the day had been, exploring the islands with Mom and Gracie hadn't taken the sting out of Brooke's escape. Maybe escape was too dramatic a word, but damn if that hadn't been how it felt. The woman had jumped off a moving boat to avoid spending the day with him. If he hadn't felt her nipples harden to firm little nubs against his chest, he might've taken that shit personally.

Oh, he knew why she took off like hell hounds were nipping at her heels. Springing his family on her had been a stupid, impulsive move. He still didn't know why he'd done it. What had felt like the perfect plan in the moment now felt like a colossal fuck up he had no idea how to rectify.

Asher surveyed the restaurant. There was a distinct lounge feel to the place. White tablecloths topped with glass. Each table had a large candle in the center, its flame protected by a surrounding vase. Soft music played through unseen speakers. Jazz or some shit. He couldn't care less about any of it. All he wanted was to find Brooke and set things right between them.

Sure, his ego had taken a serious hit when she bailed, but there was more to it than that.

Fucking *chemistry*. Time hadn't done a damn thing to lessen the explosive way his body responded to everything about her. Her taste, her touch, her sass. He couldn't explain it. Didn't have any desire to understand it. But god*damn* if he didn't want to dive in and drown himself in it.

And then what? What happens when it's time to leave again?

He hurt her before—she'd been clear on that front. Hell, he hadn't walked away unscathed, either, having her haunt his dreams over the years.

They were staying at the same resort on a small island. What the hell was he supposed to do? Pretend he didn't want to strip her naked and worship every inch of her until she went hoarse screaming his name?

Asher flexed his fingers. *Christ.* He needed a drink.

His mom and Gracie were sitting at a table on the far edge of the restaurant. He caught his mom's gaze and waved an acknowledgement. She raised an empty glass, pointed to it, then toward the bar in the back. Mom-speak for *another, please*.

Her timing couldn't have been better. Asher changed course for the bar.

"What can I get for you this evening?" the bartender greeted.

"Two Pina Colada's, one of those virgin, and a bourbon, best you got." He prayed it was better than the stuff they stocked down at Cavalier's, but at this point, he'd take what he could get.

"Make that two bourbons and put all of those drinks on my tab," a familiar voice said from behind him.

Asher gripped the edge of the bar. His stomach threatened to flip over, tightening enough to catch his breath. There was only one reason he could think of that would warrant a face-to-face while he was on leave. Shit must've hit the fan somewhere.

Asher slowly shook his head, as if with the motion he could deny the presence behind him. He had the sudden urge to hit something. Son of a *bitch*. He could already feel Mom and Gracie's disappointment when he told them he had to go. And shit. Brooke. What would she think if he disappeared again? If he left now, she'd never give him another chance. And right then, faced with the possibility of never seeing her again, Asher realized he wanted another fucking chance.

He was a selfish bastard to want anything from her when he had nothing but broken promises to give in return. He knew that. But, she got to him. A few measly hours with Brooke and he was already thinking about things he shouldn't. Like how he wanted to bash the hotel manager's face in for even looking at her.

Maybe leaving was for the best. There was a reason he

hadn't stayed in touch. Brooke was a beautiful woman who deserved better than him. She deserved a man who could be there for her, by her side through thick and thin. A man who could give her every piece of himself. A man who could put her first.

Asher hated that motherfucker already.

Where was the goddamned bourbon he ordered?

"If you need more time to finish the conversation going on in your head, Lieutenant, I can wait." There was amusement in the man's tone. "But I'm not going away."

Asher cursed inwardly. Plastering on his game face, he straightened to his full height, turned, and met the man's stare.

"Commander." Asher bobbed his chin once and shook hands with the man who had been his dad's best friend. The guy had aged well, Asher would give him that. The commander was in impeccable shape. His skin was tanned and slightly wrinkled around his mouth and eyes. His sandy blond hair had only recently begun to show signs of gray—just a hint mixed in with the blond.

Navy SEAL Commander Joel Taylor had been a staple in Asher's life. When his father died, Commander Taylor had done the best he could to be there for them through the rough patches of grief, showing up with pizza and diapers when he wasn't off somewhere saving the world.

The commander had been a major influence in Asher's decision to join the teams. He also happened to be Asher's commanding officer.

"Is there a problem, sir?"

The unease he'd been fighting all day doubled as Commander Taylor cast a glance toward the table where his mom and Gracie sat. Commander Taylor clapped a hand on his shoulder and squeezed. "Let's talk at the table."

For the first time since he turned around, Asher took note of the other man's attire. The cargo shorts weren't surprising, but the shirt with palm trees all over it was. As were the sandals.

His already fucked up day went to a whole new level of surreal.

Asher shook his head, trying to reconcile the relaxed looking guy before him with the stoic, unyielding man who commanded Naval Special Warfare Group One.

"At ease, Lieutenant. I'm not here to hijack your leave."

And the surprises kept on coming.

"What are you doing here?" While it wasn't unusual for the commander to show up at his mom's house on occasion, he'd never crashed a family vacation before. A tingling started on the back of Asher's neck.

"Grab those drinks," Commander Taylor said as he took the Pina Coladas from the bartender.

Knowing he wouldn't get an answer until the commander was good and ready to give one, Asher offered a quick thanks for the drinks, picked up the two tumblers of bourbon, and followed Commander Taylor to the table.

The commander slid into the seat next to Asher's mom. Asher took the seat across the table, next to Gracie. He pushed one of the bourbons in front of the commander, willing him to start with the explanation. The way Gracie was smiling and bouncing her legs, Asher got the feeling he was the only one in the dark.

The commander took a sip of his drink, studying him over the rim of the glass. Asher waited with the calm patience indicative of his training.

The commander lowered his glass to the table with an authoritative *thud*. "I'll skip right to the point. Your mom and I have something to discuss with you."

The tingling on his neck turned into an itch. Asher glanced between them, wondering when the commander and his mom had become a united front.

"I'm all ears, sir."

"We're getting married!" his mom blurted, her excitement spilling across the table into Gracie, who giggled and clapped her hands like she was six instead of sixteen.

Asher consulted his glass. With a sip less than two fingers remaining there was no way he was drunk, which meant...

We're getting married.

The words hung in the air like the blade of a guillotine, ready to split his family in half with the words *I do.*

A minute passed. Maybe two. Asher wasn't sure.

He didn't give a shit that the man sitting across the table was his superior, but he cared a fuck-ton that the guy had proposed to his mom, first without discussing it with him and second, knowing, *knowing* what it had done to all of them to lose his dad.

The commander had been there. Had he forgotten his mom's tears? The desperate cries for a man who would never come home again? Why in the hell would Commander Taylor want to put her in the same position again?

Anger hit Asher hard. If the commander truly loved her, he wouldn't.

"Excuse me, what?" Not that he needed to hear the words again. Asher's gaze continued to ping pong while his brain replayed them over and over in his head.

Married. Getting married. Getting. Married.

The commander slipped a hand under the table, most likely to put a meaty palm on his mom's thigh. "Ellen.

Sweetheart. We talked about this. You were going to let me talk to him first."

His mom didn't look at all chastised. "I know, Joel, and I'm sorry. Do you know how hard it's been to wait for you to arrive so we could spill the beans together?"

The hardened expression Asher had come to expect from the guy slipped. "I'm sorry I couldn't fly over with you." When he reached to brush his fingers along his mom's jawline, Asher averted his eyes skyward.

How had he not seen this coming? He knew his mom and Commander Taylor kept in touch, but he didn't know they'd been ... touching.

Jesus. Asher reached for the bourbon and brought it to his mouth for a healthy swig. "How long?" he asked through the burn.

"We've been friends for years, son. You know that."

"Friends, yes. It's the part between casual friendship and 'we're getting married' that I'm fuzzy about. How long have you been involved?"

Commander Taylor arched a brow, letting Asher know he didn't appreciate the tone. "Does it matter?"

At this point probably not, but he was becoming increasingly pissed off at being left out of the loop. He pointed an accusatory glare at Gracie. "You knew about this?"

The squirt didn't even have the decency to look guilty. "Of course I knew. I live with Mom, remember? Hard to hide a thing like that when there's a kid around."

Asher's gaze shot back to Commander Taylor. "Is that what you were trying to do? Hide?"

It was irrational for him to be angry that the commander would sneak around with his mom instead of showing her off as she deserved when he didn't want them together in the first place. Apparently, the new reality he found himself in today was a fucked up mess of contradictions.

"Asher," his mom said softly.

Watching the happiness drain from her face broke his heart in two. He'd done that. His hesitation had sucked the joy right out of her moment. As much as it killed him, her pain would be worse if she had to bury another husband.

She reached across the table and squeezed his forearm. "Don't you want me to be happy?"

Commander Taylor's frown was a good indication that now was not the time to have this conversation. But Asher and his mom were nowhere near done talking about this. Nowhere near.

"Of course I want you to be happy, Mom." It was the absolute truth.

"Then you'll give us your blessing," she said without preamble. His mom looked at the commander, then back at him. "Joel makes me happy."

Sure he did. For now. Until she remembered what life was like when she married a man who was married to the military.

Not the time.

Asher forced a smile. Unable to verbalize any type of blessing, he went with, "Have you set a date?"

At least he'd have some time to convince his mom that she could do better. The commander was as good a man as they came, but his mom deserved all of the same things Brooke deserved. Things men like him and the commander couldn't provide.

"Sunday. We wanted to have some time as newlyweds before we return to California." His mom glanced down at the table, her cheeks turning a bright crimson. Holy *Christ.* She was blushing now? Asher swallowed the rest of the bourbon, instinctively knowing he would need it to get through the rest of this conversation. His mom covered the commander's hand with hers. "We didn't know when we'd have another opportunity for all of us to be together. We didn't mean to throw this at you all at once—"

"And yet," Asher mumbled into his tumbler and Gracie kicked him under the table.

"—but I couldn't get married without my kids with me. With the unpredictability of your schedule and Joel's, we thought planning this trip, both of you taking leave, was the best way."

Asher bit his tongue, adding trickery to his mom's growing list of offenses. She must've known he'd object, otherwise she wouldn't have kept their impending nuptials a secret until now.

Sunday. What the fuck? They gave him *six days* notice?

The waiter stopped by to take their orders. Asher switched from bourbon to water. He was going to need some heavy cardio to clear his head after dinner, and running while intoxicated was a bad idea.

Gracie and his mom launched into a discussion about the wedding, details and plans yet to be made. Asher paid enough attention to nod and smile at the appropriate moments, but his real focus was on getting through the meal as quickly as he could without seeming rude.

Asher watched his mom and Commander Taylor with new eyes while they ate and the ladies planned. There was an undeniable affection between them that he could see clearly now. Sweet glances. Light touches. All the signs were right there for him to read.

While discussing the wedding, his mom continually deferred to Commander Taylor. Every time, the commander insisted she do whatever would make her happy, saying whatever she chose would make the day perfect for him as well.

Some men might say those words to get out of making decisions, but Asher knew the commander. He'd seen the man in a war room. He never flinched. Never hesitated to make a call, no matter how trivial. Commander Taylor genuinely meant it when he said his mom's happiness would ensure his own.

So, why? Why would the commander risk that happiness by offering her half a life?

Asher needed to get the hell out of there before he asked that very question. As soon as the plates were cleared and the others had ordered dessert, he didn't hesitate. He pushed away from the table.

"I'm gonna bug out."

"Where you goin'?" Gracie gave him one of her trademark sarcastic smiles. "Got a hot date?"

He immediately wondered what Brooke was doing. Was she hanging out with that Gregory guy? The thought irritated the shit out of him, but he shoved it deep.

One fucked up situation at a time, thank you very much.

Asher patted his flat, but full, stomach. "I'm going to go run off dinner before I hit the sack. It's been a long day. Are we meeting for breakfast in the morning?"

Concern pushed his mom's brows together. "We've got a lot to do the next few days. Shopping and such. Will you be okay if we leave you on your own?"

Asher couldn't help but laugh. It didn't matter how old he was, his mom would always see him as a little boy. He leaned down and kissed the top of her head. At least with Commander Taylor tagging along, Asher wouldn't have to worry about them. "I think I'll manage. Call me if you need anything."

With a goodnight to his sister and a nod to the commander, Asher tried to take his leave.

"Hold up, Lieutenant. I'll walk you out." The commander stood and jabbed a finger toward Gracie. "I'll be right back. Touch my cheesecake and you'll be grounded for life, Gracie-girl." The warning lost all heat when the guy winked, causing Gracie to laugh and wave a fork at him.

"I hear the cheesecake around here might be worth the punishment," she sang, making their mom laugh.

The ease with which Gracie accepted Commander Taylor as someone who had authority over her freedom—even in jest—spoke volumes about how clueless Asher had been.

"Then we'd better hurry," the commander said, giving Asher's shoulder a playful shove.

They fell into step, the silence tense, but not uncomfortable. Asher wasn't in the mood to chat, but he couldn't very well tell his commanding officer to fuck off, now could he? All he could do was wait to hear what the man had to say. Asher thought he might be home free as they approached the exit, but then the commander stopped him with a hand on his arm.

"You're not happy about the news."

Asher didn't bother trying to deny it. The commander would know he was lying because frankly, he was terrible at it. "As ridiculous as it sounds, it's not personal, sir."

Commander Taylor chuckled softly. "I'll keep that in mind. You want to tell me why?"

The line between the guy being his commander and his future stepfather blurred. Made his tongue loose. He blew out a frustrated breath. "You should want more for her," Asher snapped. "You can't give her what she needs."

The change was instantaneous. Warm and fuzzy groom-to-be Joel Taylor disappeared, leaving the hardened leader of men behind. The commander growled low in his throat and stepped right into Asher's space, bringing them almost chest to chest. "I can give her *everything*."

Asher wouldn't back down. Not where his family was concerned. He held the commander's stare. Didn't fucking blink. "Yeah. I'll bet that's what my dad thought, too."

A fury contained by years of practice and discipline fired in the commander's eyes. It was obvious the commander wanted to take a swing at him, and Asher almost wished he would. At least then something about his day would make sense.

As it was, he made his point. He needed to go before something happened that either jeopardized his job or brought his mom and sister running. Or both.

He turned to leave. "Enjoy your cheesecake, Commander."

7

BROOKE STRETCHED out on the double lounger and listened to the waves as they lapped at the shore. The night air had a mild chill, one that made her glad she traded her swimsuit for a pair of loose cotton sleep shorts and an oversized tee. The only light on the patio came from the three-wicked candle on the small table next to her. The gentle breeze off the water made the trio of flames dance, creating moving shadows all around her. The rich navy sky was dotted with stars, too many to even think about counting. It was, quite simply, the most beautiful night she'd ever experienced.

A contented sigh slipped from her lips as she took a sip of wine—the same vintage she had that afternoon at Seafare. A gift from Gregory, sent over an hour ago with his thanks for sharing a meal and for the work she'd be doing.

Brooke couldn't resist opening the bottle even if she didn't have anyone to share it with. She considered inviting Ash to have a drink with her until she remembered she didn't have his phone or room number. Hanging out in the resort common areas waiting to see if he walked by so she could issue an invitation seemed a little too pathetic for her taste. She'd rather drink alone, thank you very much.

And anyway, she was supposed to be annoyed with him. She wanted to be annoyed with him, but the way they moved together on that boat ... *Holy crackers.* Her body had been in a state of constant arousal since then. Instead of focusing on the work she was there to do, Asher's veiled threat of retribution played on a loop in her mind, thoroughly distracting her.

She tried. She really did. She spent the entire afternoon lying on the beach, working possible angles for the ad campaign. All she ended up with was a sunburn and a driving need to shove her hand into her shorts to work off her insane fantasies featuring one sexy Navy SEAL.

Brooke groaned into her glass.

If only she didn't remember how *good* they'd been together. The perfect way he'd touched her, filled her. The cabana was proof positive their chemistry was combustible. And oh, she wanted to *burn*.

Brooke finished off the wine with one hand while she reached for the open bottle with the other.

I'll be coming to collect.

His words were like a physical stroke down her body, leaving heat in their wake. She could still feel the puff of his breath against her skin. The raw power of his kiss. Brooke squeezed her thighs together, willing the ache that had taken up residence in her core to ease.

Brooke refilled her glass and took another long drink. The wine infused her veins, adding to the warmth already coursing through her.

She should let him. Collect, that is. She wasn't thrilled with how he'd up and left her all those years ago, but the past was the past. As she told him, she hadn't expected them to be more than friends in the long run anyway. Why should now be any different? She wanted him. It was pretty obvious he wanted her, too. They were both single adults. What was the harm in having a little fun?

The sound of the waves coupled with the wine made her feel blissfully relaxed. *Reckless.* So much so, she was able to ignore the ache in her chest at the idea of starting something with him that again had an obvious expiration date.

Two weeks. A little less, actually, before she left Grand Turks and returned home.

Brooke set her glass on the table next to the wine bottle. She reclined against the back of the chair and closed her eyes.

Asher didn't want anything long-term? Fine. Maybe she didn't either. She hadn't exactly been successful at the relationship thing anyway. The last guy she dated had lasted three weeks before he started complaining about how much she worked. As though ambition was a bad thing. A couple of weeks after that, he stopped calling. She hadn't lost a moment of sleep. Her work was important to her. So was the stability her income provided. She had a modest apartment in a nice area of San Diego, food in her refrigerator, and the assurance that the electricity would be on whenever she got home—things her mom's flighty behavior ensured Brooke could never take for granted as a child. Brooke had sworn once she was old enough to earn her own money, she'd do whatever it took to make sure she never had to worry about basic needs again. Her job gave her more than security. It gave her peace of mind.

Counting on another person hadn't worked out so well for her. All she had was herself. White picket fence, marriage, children... Those weren't things she wasted time dreaming about. That didn't mean she wanted to spend her life alone. She didn't. If she was going to be with a man for any length of time, he would have to be a man secure enough with himself, and with her, for those times they were apart. She liked her independence. She'd been on her own too long to suddenly give up the reins. She didn't think she could be with a man who would ask her to.

"What are you doing out here?"

Brooke surged up, a tiny shout leaping from her mouth. She clutched at her chest, her heart racing a mile a minute. Apparently, she drank more wine than she thought, because the world swayed a little.

"Jesus. Asher." She glanced up. Blinked, then blinked again. Not just Asher. A half-naked, glistening with sweat Asher. And *whoa*. Hello, abs.

Brooke chewed her bottom lip. He'd been fit when they were together before, but not like he was now. She'd had her hands all over his body, and then she'd dreamed of him enough that she thought she had him memorized.

She was wrong.

The man standing over her no longer wore the body of a twenty-something man, but one seasoned with age and hard work. Triumph and tragedy were etched into every honed muscle, every dip and valley his body had to offer. And oh lord, her hands itched to map every inch of this new territory.

As she apparently had with the wine, Brooke over-indulged in the sight of him. As one should when presented with such a display of perfectly sculpted male flesh, Brooke took her time, leisurely exploring the feast of bared skin above her. Her gaze dipped down and back up again until she landed on what appeared to be a recently healed injury on his shoulder. She was about to ask him what happened when his hands landed on his hips, drawing her attention to the mouth-watering vee that dipped and disappeared behind the waistband of his shorts.

"You done?"

Brooke ignored his snippy tone. "Oh, please. If I showed up on your patio all sweaty and without my shirt, you'd look, too."

"If you showed up topless on my patio, I promise you, I'd be doing a whole lot more than looking." His heated stare looked almost sinister in the shadows of the candlelight. "I asked you a question. What are you doing out here? Alone. In the dark."

She waved a hand to indicate her lounging body and the table holding the wine. "What does it look like I'm doing?"

"It looks like you've been drinking and are about to fall asleep out in the open where anyone can get to you."

A smile tugged at her lips. Maybe it made her a terrible person, but she liked that he worried about her, even if it was only due to his natural protective instincts.

"You worry too much."

"You don't worry enough."

Brooke let out an exaggerated sigh, just to annoy him. "Why are you here, Ash?"

Ash dropped down on the chair and stretched out beside her.

"What are you drinking?" He reached across her body. His arm unapologetically grazed her chest as he grabbed her wine glass from the table, causing her breath to catch. He smelled like the ocean, his skin salty with sweat. Brooke had to force herself not to press her face into his neck and make that scent her own.

He brought the glass to his lips, so close her nose almost brushed his cheek. Watching his throat work, Brooke was unable to do anything but swallow along with him. She wondered how the wine would taste coming from his mouth. She could find out. A tilt of her chin and she could lick—

Asher's face scrunched. His over-the-top grimace snapped her out of her musings. She stuttered a laugh. "That's what you get for stealing my drink."

He looked truly affronted as he put the glass back where he found it and settled back into place beside her. "What is that crap?"

Now that he wasn't leaning over her, Brooke could breathe a little easier. "It's chardonnay. Gregory ordered it at lunch and I enjoyed it so much he sent over a bottle."

Asher sneered toward the ocean. "He didn't deliver it personally?"

What was with the attitude?

"No," Brooke said slowly, taking in his hardened profile. If she didn't know any better, she'd think he was jealous. "Someone from Guest Services brought it over with a note."

"What did it say?"

She studied him, curious as to the reason for his mood. "He thanked me for having lunch with him and indicated he was excited about the new campaign."

Asher hummed as if there were more to it than that.

"What? Gregory is a nice man."

He hummed again, only this time his lips thinned. Brooke had no idea why he was being so weird. Or why she felt the need to explain. "It's a bottle of wine between colleagues. It doesn't mean anything. Clients send me thank you gifts all the time. It's not a big deal. There's more in the bottle. If you want some, help yourself."

His gaze found hers then, pinning her to the chair with its intensity. "You're inviting me to stay? After that shit you pulled this morning, I wasn't sure I'd even be welcome."

76

"Of course you're welcome." She was too relaxed to ruin it by talking about how he'd blindsided her. "Besides, I've had a good day." If by good she meant being distracted and unproductive. "I'm feeling generous."

He folded his hands over his tight stomach, wiggling his shoulders as though settling in. He dropped his head to lay against the back of the chair, his stare pointed toward the night sky. "I'm glad your day's been good, because mine's been a shit storm."

Because of her? "Do you want to talk about it?"

He rolled his head to look at her, one arrogant brow lifted. "I'm more interested in finding out how far this generosity of yours extends."

Although she had already decided to sleep with him, Brooke had consumed just enough wine to want to make him work for it. If they were going to fuck, he had to give her something besides orgasms. Something real. A tiny piece of himself that she could take with her when they parted ways. It was only fair.

When she tried to sit up, Ash's fingers wrapped around her forearm, holding her in place. "Don't take off again," he murmured. "I've just finished a ten-mile run. If you go, I will come after you. I'm beat, so if you make me do that, there will be consequences."

The threat wasn't exactly a good deterrent. She knew firsthand that being on the receiving end of his "consequences" would be well worth the chase. As tempting as the notion might be, she had no intention of running from him tonight.

"Where am I going to go? This is my patio." When he held tight, she added, "I'm not going anywhere." He squeezed her arm once—a warning she felt from her nipples to her sex—before letting go. She sat up and turned around to face him. She tugged at her shorts, straightening things up before she crossed her legs. "What happened? Tell me about your day."

"Mmm." He looked her over. "I like this position much better." He slid his palm across her knee. He splayed his fingers and started a slow ascent of her bare thigh. "My day might've sucked, but my night is looking up."

"We're in paradise. How bad could it have been?"

"It didn't start out that way." His thumb bypassed the edge of her shorts, caressing the crease where her thigh and hip met. "In fact, it started off great."

Brooke knew the exact moment he realized she wasn't wearing panties. His nostrils flared and his grip on her hip tightened to the point that she glanced down. The sight of his long, perfectly shaped fingers wrapped around her thigh made her head spin. A thrum built between her legs, ramping up her breath and her heartbeat.

"Is…" She couldn't stop staring at his hand, wondering what his next move would be. She licked her lips and started again. "Is that right?"

His thumb swept across her skin, back and forth, back and forth, each swipe inching him closer to her mound. "Yep. The hottest girl I've ever seen let me kiss her in an empty cabana."

"Lucky you." *I'll let you kiss me on the patio, too. Kiss me.*

Asher stared at her mouth as if she'd said the words aloud. "You'd think, right? But within minutes of that kiss, she ditched me."

Before she knew what was happening, Asher gripped her forearm and tugged her over his lap. She barely had time to brace herself before he gave her ass a resounding *smack*.

"Hey!" she jumped and laughingly struggled to sit up.

He pressed an arm against her lower back, holding her still as he popped her other cheek.

"You think this is funny?" His brow went up at the same time as his hand, as if both were controlled by the same unseen force.

The wine gave her a case of the giggles. "Stop! Stop! I'm sorry, okay? You surprised me with the impromptu family introductions. I panicked."

"You won't do it again."

"Do what?"

"Panic. Say it, Brooke. Say you won't run from me again. At least not without an explanation and an opportunity to talk you out of it."

"I..."

His hand came down and she tensed, squeezing her eyes shut, waiting for the sting that never came. She gasped as the warmth of his palm caressed up the back of her thigh, slipping under her shorts to squeeze the bare skin of her ass.

"You're killing me, you know that? C'mere."

He helped her sit up, then he urged one of her legs over, encouraging her to straddle his lap. Still feeling a buzz, Brooke held onto his shoulders as she tilted her head back, giving her loose hair a little shake to get it out of her eyes. Feeling the need for wicked revenge, she widened her knees and brought her hips down.

"Damn it." He growled as she rocked against the solid length of him. "I didn't come here for this." His fingers bit into the flesh of her thighs close, so close, to where she wanted him.

"Then why did you come?"

"I didn't plan it." His voice sounded tortured. "I had dinner with the family and..." He hesitated long enough to remind her that she wanted to know what happened tonight.

"And?" she prompted. Dying for a taste of him, Brooke leaned in and pressed her lips against his collarbone. A quick flick of her tongue wasn't enough. She needed more.

"I needed to clear my head, so I went for a run. I just kind of ended up here." He groaned as she nipped the skin on the side of his neck. "*Fuck*. Brooke. You said you didn't want this, yet you're practically begging to be fucked right here where anyone walking down the beach could see."

She froze. That wouldn't do. It was bad enough he ran shirtless for every woman at the resort to drool over. She had no desire to share the rest of him.

"So, take me inside."

Her plan for revenge backfired in a big way, because she was the one burning up. The wine. The spanking. His big cock hard, for her. Because of her. It was all too much. She squeezed his hips between her thighs. "Please, Asher."

She squeaked as Asher cupped her backside. With a strength that shocked her, Asher twirled them around and surged to his feet with her in his arms.

"Let's go."

SOMETIMES DOING the right thing wasn't easy. It was made harder still when the sexy as fuck woman riding the shape of his dick like a pro jockey was the one he'd spent years trying to forget.

Par for the course of his fucked up day. Maybe he was still sleeping off last night's bourbon. Any minute now he'd wake up. Learn his mom and the commander weren't getting married, and the girl he'd almost loved and definitely lost wasn't back in his arms where it felt like she belonged.

Maybe he should've run twenty miles, because it seemed ten hadn't been enough to get his ass-backward head on straight.

He carried Brooke toward the door. She'd left the slider open, something he was equally grateful for and annoyed about. Grateful because he wouldn't have to let her go—something he wasn't ready to do—in order to deal with the door. Annoyed that she'd been reckless enough to leave herself vulnerable.

What if it hadn't been him who showed up tonight? What if it had been that asshole from the bar, looking to finish what he started?

Asher flexed his fingers, digging into the flesh he held. She needed to be more careful.

"Ash." Brooke's fingers along his jaw line made him realize his teeth were clenched. He relaxed his jaw as she pressed her forehead against his.

Her eyes were glassy and bright, making him wish he'd checked the contents of the wine bottle to gauge just how much she'd had to drink. This close, he could smell the fruity scent on her breath.

"What is it, baby?"

"Where'd you go?"

He shook his head. That was yet another conversation that would have to wait. He couldn't explain safety to her while she was looking at him through her thick eyelashes and chewing her goddamn lip like she was seconds from coming and he was the only one who could get her there.

Full disclosure time.

"You should know, I'm not going to fuck you tonight."

Brooke's hips stopped the maddening grind and her

back went stiff. Her arms loosened from around his neck, but it didn't matter. He had her, and he wasn't planning to let go. Not yet, anyway.

"Brooke..."

Indignation flared in her eyes. "Put me down."

"Not a chance."

"If you don't want me..." Her cheeks flamed. "God, this is stupid. Let. Me. Go."

She struggled until he had two choices: drop her onto the bed or the floor. He picked the mattress. She bounced once and he advanced on her, over her, situating himself between her spread thighs. His forward momentum forced her onto her back as he braced himself on his palms above her.

God, she was sexy. Cerulean eyes, heavy-lidded and hungry. Her lip swollen from where she'd bit, her cheeks flushed, her hair in wild disarray.

Good intentions went out the window and he did the only thing he could do in that precise moment. He took her mouth, fast and fierce. Punishing. She thought he didn't want her? Didn't she know he was fucking choking with the need to yank those flimsy shorts aside and bury himself deep? He'd been ready for her since the moment he'd first seen her in the bar, even before he realized who she was.

Brooke whimpered into his mouth and Asher eased back, giving them both time to catch their breath. "There is nothing stupid about the way I'm feeling right now. Nothing at all."

Asher ran a hand up the outside of her thigh, loving the feel of her silky smooth skin against his palm. He slid around to cup her backside, pulling her tight against him. He shoved his aching prick against her folds. Hot. So fucking hot.

"Feel how hard I am? That's all for you."

"Then let me have it."

Christ. This woman. "No."

"Why not?"

Her sexy pout damn near made him change his mind. Who did he need to see about sainthood? Because after this, he damn sure should qualify.

"For starters? Just this morning you told me this wasn't what you wanted."

Her fingers trailed down his spine, weakening his resolve with every vertebra. He had to shut this down. Now.

"I'm not allowed to change my mind?"

Asher shook his head. "Not when I can't be sure it's you talking and not the alcohol. Which brings me to reason number two, and, for the record, the sole reason I'm not buried to the hilt inside your hot little body right now. You've been drinking."

She arched, rubbing her breasts against his chest. "I'm not drunk." She scrunched her nose and giggled. "Although, I'll admit I had more wine I thought."

"You're so fucking cute right now." Tipsy or drunk... whatever the adjective, it didn't matter. He would not take a woman to bed who'd been drinking unless she consented while sober. Brooke had not. He made her regret him once before. He wouldn't do it again. "And stop rubbing on me like you're a cat. I'm having a hard enough time keeping my hands off you as it is."

"Then, don't. Touch me. I want you to touch me."

Asher groaned. She was not making this easy for him. "Brooke." Her breathing hitched as he lowered down, bringing them nose to nose. "Listen up, sassy girl. The next time I get inside you, I want you stone-cold sober. I don't want any doubts or regrets between us. Only desire and pleasure." He pressed his hips into hers one more time to drive the point home. There would be pleasure. So fucking much.

The lust shining in her eyes told him she knew it, too.

Soon, he silently promised. *Soon.*

Right now it was time to go, before his moral compass spun in the wrong direction.

"You owe me a day. Tomorrow. Just you and me." He rubbed the tip of her nose with his. "Tell me what I want to hear, sweetheart."

She stretched up, a sensual smile curving her lips before they brushed against his.

"Yes."

Best fucking word, ever.

8

BROOKE WOKE WITH A HEADACHE, thanks to the half bottle of wine she consumed the night before. She knew the amount because the bottle was on the counter in the kitchen, along with a bottle of ibuprofen and a note from Asher indicating she should meet him in the lobby later that morning for their "date."

Day, not date, she reminded herself. Regardless of the term Asher used, they weren't dating. Would never date. She couldn't have her heart getting confused about what was going on between them.

She took an extra long shower. She didn't bother with makeup since her skin held a healthy glow from yesterday's sun. She towel dried and braided her hair. She felt almost human as she donned a long dress and sandals. Without knowing what he had planned for the day, Brooke was unsure what she should wear. She thought about calling him to check, then immediately got irritated because she still didn't know what room he was in or have his phone number. She resolved to remedy that situation when she saw him again.

Using the slider, Brooke stepped outside and into what promised to be a beautiful day. She double checked to make sure the lock re-engaged before heading toward the main building. The dining room located within the lobby offered an extensive Bloody Mary bar. Some eggs, bacon, and a Bloody Mary with all the trimmings would be just the ticket to get her on the right track. She didn't want a headache to ruin her day with Asher.

God. Asher.

She couldn't believe she'd thrown herself at him last night. Brooke snorted at the thought. She was giving herself too much credit. Throwing herself at him would've been slightly less embarrassing than the dry humping routine she performed when he carried her inside. And that wasn't even the worst part. She was the one who wanted something real from him. The minute an opportunity presented itself to do just that, she turned into some kind of drunken, lap dancing hussy and ignored the reason he sought her out in lieu of what was in his pants. It served her right that she had been left wanting on both counts.

"How many?" the girl behind the hostess stand asked as Brooke approached.

She had over an hour before she was supposed to meet Asher. His note hadn't said anything about breakfast and there was no way she could function without some food in her belly. She'd brought her laptop along so she could get some work done while she ate.

"One, please."

The hostess smiled. "Right this way."

The girl led Brooke to a table for four. While she could use the extra table space to work, she didn't want to take up unnecessary room so close to the peak breakfast hour. The restaurant was quite busy.

"I can wait for a smaller table if you have a group that could use this one."

The hostess looked surprised. "While I appreciate your offer, it's not necessary. You shouldn't have to wait simply because you are dining alone this morning. We like to make sure all of our guests get the same consideration." She set a menu on the table. "Your server will be by to take your order. Enjoy your breakfast."

Less than five minutes later, with her breakfast order taken and a Bloody Mary in front of her, Brooke dug her laptop and notebook out of her bag.

She reviewed her notes from the day before, crossing out most of the ideas she'd played around with on the beach. She needed something with impact. Something that would bring meaning to the grand opening of the couples resort.

Brooke picked up her pen and wrote *destination weddings* on the paper. They were all the rage these days. Weddings, honeymoons, renewal of vows. What better way to target the couple market than to offer wedding packages? The Midnight Bay Couples Resort would forever be etched into the minds of those who were bound in matrimony there. Those couples would return to relive the magic. They would tell all their friends about their amazing wedding, the friendliness of the staff, and the stunning beauty of Turks and Caicos.

Perfect.

Brooke brainstormed on paper and the foundation for a new campaign began to form. Her scrambled eggs with cheese and a side of bacon were delivered and she made several lists while she ate. Potential ideas for the kinds of photographs she would need for the pitch. Target markets they would hit. Questions to ask Gregory, since he hadn't mentioned offering any type of wedding or honeymoon packages.

"Excuse me. Brooke?"

Startled from her work, it took Brooke a minute for her brain to process the fact that Asher's sister was standing next to the table.

"Oh. Grace. I...I, um..." Brooke looked around for Asher. If he'd set her up again, she would have his balls in a vise before lunch.

"My brother's not here," Grace told her. "I haven't seen him yet, but then again, Mom and I didn't make plans with him today since we have to go shopping. Do you mind if I sit?"

Since Grace had pulled out the chair next to her and was already half way onto it, Brooke figured the question was rhetorical, but she answered anyway.

"Sure, but could you give me a minute? I need to finish this one thing." She quickly finished jotting down the hook she'd been working on, then gathered the notes she had spread out all over the table.

"What'cha working on?" Grace's eager, somewhat mischievous smile was achingly familiar. It was the same smile Asher had flashed her way before their trek down the beach yesterday. Brooke felt an instant connection to the girl. Under different circumstances, they might have become good friends.

Not for the first time, Brooke wondered what it would be like to have a sister. She had girlfriends, but none she would consider close. In school, she was too busy studying and taking care of things around the house. She didn't have the time or energy required to nurture friendships. As an adult, she worked all the time. The few friends she'd managed to hang on to worked as hard as she did.

"An advertising campaign for a new section of this resort that opens next year."

Grace's eyes bugged. "You work here? That's so cool."

Brooke chuckled as she stuffed papers into her bag. "No, but I agree it would be totally cool to work and live here. As things are though, I work for an agency in San Diego. They sent me here to get the lay of the land and meet with the guy in charge."

"You live in San Diego, then?"

It was surreal, being interrogated by the teenaged sister of the guy she'd begged to fuck her last night. "Yes. North Park."

Grace toyed with the edge of the table cloth. "I guess that's where you met my brother?"

"Actually, no. I used to live in Coronado. That's where we met." Brooke didn't have a lot—or any—experience with teenagers, other than having been one herself once. Did they all take so long to get to the point? Because Brooke was sure Grace had one. She hadn't stopped by for the hell of it.

Brooke didn't want to be rude, but neither could she afford to get attached. She sensed the longer she spent with Asher's sister, the more the girl would grow on her. Was already growing on her.

"Is there something you wanted to——"

"I'm sorry," Grace blurted, her cheeks blooming pink. "I shouldn't have been so rude to you yesterday. Ash didn't tell us about you. I was surprised and..."

"Hurt?" Brooke guessed.

"Jealous." Grace's face scrunched. "That sounds so petty, wanting to hog him all to myself. I'm sure you don't get to see him any more than I do, considering he's gone all the time. Asher wasn't happy that I ran you off yesterday. Do you hate me?"

Brooke wasn't surprised that Grace had been jealous, but she was taken aback that a girl of sixteen would so willingly admit such a thing. Coupled with the apology, it was clear Grace was mature for her age. Brooke would need to be on her toes around this one, lest she forget Grace was, in fact, still quite young.

No. You don't need to be on your toes, because you're not going to be a part of her life. Don't forget that.

Be that as it may, Grace was Asher's sister. She couldn't let the girl think she was upset with her when she wasn't.

"Of course I don't hate you. *You* didn't do anything wrong. Can I let you in on a little secret?" When Grace nodded vigorously, Brooke said, "I was surprised, too. I knew you and your mom were on the island, but I didn't know you'd be on the boat yesterday. The reason I left had nothing to do with you, so please, don't give it another thought. And since I owe you an apology for the way I bailed, how about we call it even? Start over with a clean slate?"

Before Grace could answer, Gregory appeared. "Ms. Ramsey." He smiled. "Brooke. I'm glad I saw you sitting there." He glanced between her and Grace. "My apologies for the interruption. Might I have a word? It won't take but a moment."

It seemed apologies were a dime a dozen this morning. "Grace, do you mind? Gregory is the man I'm working with here at the resort."

Grace's cheeks turned the color of a fire engine. She was staring at Gregory as if the man held the secrets of the universe and he planned to share them at any moment. "I, um, no. I don't mind."

Brooke gestured toward an empty chair, which Gregory was quick to claim.

90

"Is everything all right?" she asked.

"Yes. Yes, of course. Everything is fine. I had a brilliant idea I couldn't wait to share with you. As you know, we will be offering private romantic dinners for our couples at the new location. In order for you to understand what we are trying to accomplish, I've made arrangements for you and your boyfriend to have dinner in one of the new spaces this evening, if that works for your schedule. If not, we can pick another night."

Brooke cringed at the word *boyfriend*. She snuck a quick glance toward Grace, who was watching the interaction with rapt attention.

Great. Asher had introduced her to Grace as his friend. Maybe Grace would assume Brooke had traveled with someone else. But what if Asher mentioned to Grace that he was having dinner with her? Then Grace would think they were together. Grace would certainly tell her mom and ... how the hell had everything gotten so fucking complicated?

That's why it was always better to be honest. You tell one lie, even a lie of omission, and it snowballed out of control. She should just come clean. Tell Gregory that she and Asher weren't a couple and stop this farce right now. It wasn't as if the guy actually cared whether or not they were together.

"Gregory," she started, intending to set him straight, but the man talked right over her.

"Of course, the kitchen there isn't ready for meal preparation, but Chef Rancourt jumped at the chance to cook for you. He will prepare your meal at Seafare, but you will be served at the new location in the same fashion as our guests will be after we open. Isn't that fantastic?"

"Isn't what fantastic?" a familiar voice boomed from behind her. "Gracie, what are you doing here?"

Not again. Brooke groaned.

There wasn't enough ibuprofen on the island for the headache rebuilding inside Brooke's skull. She turned to glare at the man who had started all of this.

Asher looked good, damn him. His hair was shining, wet from a shower or maybe a morning swim. He wore a white short-sleeved button-up tucked into black shorts. He was even wearing a belt. He looked more ready to play golf than spend the day on the beach.

"Never mind about Grace," she snapped. "What are *you* doing here?"

He frowned. "You're late. I warned you I'd come looking."

"I'm not late on purpose." She tilted her head toward the others at the table. "As you can see, I got distracted."

Ever helpful, Gregory stood and clapped Asher on the shoulder. "I was just explaining to Brooke that I planned a quiet, romantic dinner for the two of you tonight."

Annnnd they were outta there.

Brooke surged up from her chair. "Didn't you say we were late?" She grabbed her laptop and shoved it into her bag. "We'd better get a move on. Grace, it was nice chatting with you. Gregory, I ..." *Need to get the hell out of here before the start of Grace Interrogation: Round Two.* "Can I get back to you? Thanks."

Brooke didn't wait for an answer. She hooked her arm around Asher's and all but dragged him out of the restaurant. And she kept right on going until they were out of the hotel and on the path that led to her room.

"You wanna tell me what that was back there?" Asher asked, his long strides easily keeping up with her accelerated pace. "Why were you and my sister together? And what's this about a romantic dinner? Brooke. Goddamn it. Will you *stop*?" He jerked her around to face him, his hands cradling her biceps as though he wanted to shake her. "What's lit that fire under your ass?"

Brooke shook her head and chuckled, softly at first. The last forty-eight hours had definitely been the most interesting of her life. Douchebag Brett. Asher, pretending to be her boyfriend. Asher, whose concerned look said he might be questioning her current mental state.

Then, there was the fact that he was even there, on the same island, thousands of miles from where either of them called home. Meeting his family. Grace and her apology. Gregory and his romantic dinner planning.

The ridiculousness of the entire situation hit her all at once. Asher Dillon had shown up and turned her life upside down. Again. What were the fucking odds?

In all the gin joints...

Brooke broke into a serious case of the giggles. She laughed until tears blurred her vision.

"What's so funny?" Asher demanded.

"I'm ..." She waved a hand, dislodging his from her arm. "Gimme a sec."

The good news was the laughter released all the tension in her body, making her feel almost refreshed. The bad news was that Asher would probably cancel their day together after she finished acting like a lunatic.

She giggle-groaned and held her palms against her aching side. "Sorry. It's just..." She swallowed hard, trying to keep the giggles at bay. "Your sister now thinks we're a couple."

The hardened look on Asher's face dried her humor right up.

"Why are you looking at me like that?"

"I'm trying to decide if I should be offended or just

downright pissed off that you find the idea of being tied to me so hilarious."

Huh? "I wasn't laughing because I thought us being a couple was funny. I was laughing about the fact that our lie-by-omission-pretend-relationship has grown legs and learned to walk. And why would you be offended or angry anyway? Didn't you recently explain to me, in detail, how you refuse to be tied to anyone?"

"Yeah. I guess I did."

"All right, then." Brooke tilted her head and studied him. He didn't look appeased. She smoothed the front of his shirt, even though it didn't need it. When she got to his belt, she hooked her finger through one of the loops and gave it a little tug. "Let it go, champ."

He stepped closer. "Knots."

"What?"

"My nickname isn't 'champ.' It's Knots. That's what my SEAL buddies call me."

Realization dawned. "I get it. Clever. Knots, as in nautical miles, right?"

He closed the distance between them. One hand came to rest on the curve of her hip. With the other, he reached around and took hold of her braid. He gave it a pull, forcing her to raise her chin to meet his heated gaze.

"As in rope." *Oh.* "I have you to thank, actually, since my proficiency in tying knots started with you."

Holy crackers. Heat crept into her face.

"You're so damn pretty when you blush like that." He released her braid and cupped the side of her face. His thumb stroked across her cheek. "You're thinking about it right now, aren't you?" He groaned. "All those times I used your scarves to—"

Brooke pressed two fingers across his lips. The visions

swimming around in her head were enough to make her panties uncomfortably damp. If she had to listen to him describe what they'd done together, she might combust.

"You should call Grace and explain the situation to her before she tells your mom," Brooke said to get them back on track. "I'm going to assume from our conversation the other night that you haven't introduced a woman to your family before. I would hate for them to get the wrong idea and then be disappointed when they learn the truth."

Asher let her go with a sigh. "You'd be right about that. I've never brought a girl home, not even when I was in high school. But, don't worry about it. I'll handle Gracie, and if need be, my mom. They have enough to distract them today. Gracie probably won't even remember what was said."

"What are they doing today?"

He shook his head. "Later. Tell me about the dinner Meeks mentioned. What's the story?"

Brooke wondered if those distractions were the reason he came to see her last night. She made a mental note to circle back to that topic.

"Come on. I need to drop my stuff off in the room before we head out. I'll explain on the way. We do still have plans today, right?"

"Yep. By the way, that dress is sexy as all get out. I love the way it hugs your curves."

His husky tone made her shiver. Brooke glanced down at her blue and white tie-dyed sundress, pleased that he liked what he saw and wasn't afraid to let her know. The least she could do was remind him that they were on the same page.

"Play your cards right, *Knots*, and my dress won't be the only thing hugging my curves."

9

THE DAY HAD BEEN PERFECT. Too perfect. As in his-chest-was-tight-while-he-waited-for-the bubble-to-burst perfect.

Asher had chartered a boat for the afternoon. They explored the various islands, had a picnic lunch with their guide aboard the boat, and then snorkeled until the sun began to set. By the time they headed back to the hotel to get ready for dinner, Asher had started to rethink his reasons for avoiding the water outside of work.

Being with Brooke made him feel lighter somehow. Less jaded, more willing to try anything if it meant seeing her smile or hearing her laugh. It was crazy. They fucked every day for a month, didn't see each other for eight years, and he'd only just seen her again three days ago. *Three days.* Apparently that was all the time it took, because if he was half in love with her before, he was well on his way to finishing the job now.

He didn't know how to stop the runaway train that was headed right for them.

So, there he was, freshly showered and dressed in his favorite dress shirt and slacks, standing outside Brooke's door, ready to take her for a romantic dinner. And he was fucking *nervous*.

Asher pumped his fists, working blood into his shaking fingers. The nerves freaked him the hell out. He'd faced enemies in battle with less activity in his gut. So, why did the idea of taking one gorgeous, tiny woman to dinner feel so ... *significant*?

You're being an idiot. People don't fall in love in three days. It feels significant because you've been hard for her all day. You and your dick both know the wait will soon be over.

Right. Okay. What he was feeling had nothing to do with significance. It was anticipation. Nothing more. He could work with that.

Work on knocking on the door, dumbass.

"I can hear you shuffling around out there. Are you planning to knock anytime soon?" Brooke's voice drifted through the door. "I'm hungry."

The sound of her voice calmed him. It also made seeing her an urgent matter. He rapped a knuckle against the door. "Open up, gorgeous. Dinner awaits."

The door flew open and it took him a second to speak. Her sun-drenched hair was down, framing her like a goddamn halo. She wore another sundress, this one a silvery blue that shimmered in the light and set off her ever-deepening tan. The dress fit tightly around her breasts and waist, only to flare out into a skirt that barely reached her mid-thigh. And her shoes ... Asher groaned. Strappy white sandals. They were ultra-feminine, delicate-looking with a long thin heel that made her bare legs look miles long.

Christ Almighty. He wanted to fuck her in nothing but those shoes.

"Ash?"

When he opened his mouth, the words that came out didn't seem enough. "You are stunning."

Brooke crossed her ankles, fanned out her skirt, and gave him an adorable, playful curtsy. "Thank you. And don't you look handsome."

She reached out to smooth the front of his shirt, a growing habit she seemed to enjoy. Instinctively, he leaned in, not only accepting her touch, but encouraging her to continue.

She trailed a fingernail over his buttons, one by one. "How many dress shirts did you pack?" she asked with a sly smile.

How was he supposed to come up with a number with her hands on him? If she kept with the petting, they'd never make it to dinner. "I dunno. Five or six, I guess."

Her smile grew. "Don't most men pack shorts and T-shirts when they go on vacation?"

"I wouldn't know what other men pack." He flattened her wandering hand against his chest, right over his heart.

It occurred to him how little they actually knew about each other. So far, they'd kept the conversation light. No deep diving into each other's thoughts and lives. It was his standard MO. He met, he seduced, he fucked, he said good-bye. No muss, no fuss. With one exception: Brooke. She was different. She made *him* want to be different.

He tucked a piece of hair behind her ear, loving the feel of the silky smooth waves against his fingers. "Some fun facts about me, Brooke. I love good bourbon and nice clothes." His SEAL buddies loved to give him shit about both. "I'm more comfortable wearing slacks than wearing jeans that cut off my circulation. My junk needs room to breathe."

At the mention of his cock, Brooke's gaze dipped as if to

see for herself. He died a little when she licked her lips. Fuck him, there was no way he could handle her checking him out so blatantly when they had to go.

He put a knuckle under her chin and lifted her gaze back to his. "As I was saying." He cleared the gravel from his throat. "I prefer slacks. I like shirts with buttons, long-sleeved and short. You should know that I also packed a suit." Which, as it turns out, had been a good decision. He didn't have his dress uniform. If his mom insisted on going through with the wedding, at least he wouldn't look like a total tool for the photos.

"But don't worry," Asher went on to reassure her. "I brought several T-shirts and pairs of board shorts for swimming. I even brought a pair of jeans and an old pair of sweats that I wear sometimes while I'm chilling on the couch."

"Are you saying you're not always this neat and clean?"

Asher laughed and pulled her into his arms. He breathed her in, and God, she smelled amazing. Her coconut scent went straight to his head. "You saw me last night, right? After my run? There wasn't anything *neat* or *clean* about me then."

He brought his face close, his lips grazing her ear. "But, I'd be happy to remind you of how dirty I can get." In truth, he would love nothing more than to strip her down and taste every inch of her body, but that would have to wait. Brooke's client had arranged dinner for them and Asher would be damned if they were going to insult the man or jeopardize her work reputation by showing up late.

He nipped the outer edge of Brooke's ear, growling in satisfaction at her sharp intake of breath. "But, not right now. We've got to go, sweetheart."

He felt her feather-light whisper against the hollow of his throat. "Later, then."

"Later." If he tasted her lips, they'd never get out of there, so he kissed her forehead instead, sealing the promise of things to come.

GREGORY HAD ARRANGED FOR EVERYTHING. A staff member met them outside the lobby and drove them over to the new resort in a four-seater golf cart. When the driver skirted around the buildings and headed for the beach, Brooke leaned forward.

"Are you sure this is the way?" She thought they would be eating in one of the new restaurant spaces.

"Yes, ma'am. It's just over there." The driver pointed to an area of the beach that seemed to be glowing.

"Wow." Asher whistled low as the spot came into view. "Isn't that something?"

Brooke couldn't believe the beauty of it. Ground level torches lit a pathway toward a cabana, much like the one where Asher had kissed her, only smaller. More intimate.

Brooke went into work mode, mentally cataloguing every detail.

Surrounded by a square of taller torches than the ones used on the path, the cabana's sheer curtains were pulled back to reveal a table, two chairs, and the vast expanse of the ocean as a backdrop.

There was no music to discourage conversation, just the rolling *shush* of the ocean as it moved. There was no other activity going on to distract the couple—them, for tonight—from each other.

There were two employees dressed in black and white

uniforms standing to the left of the path, and Brooke wondered if they would hang around or make themselves scarce once their meal had been served.

Guess she was about to find out.

Asher helped her out of the golf cart. Once she was standing, he glanced down at her feet with a cringe. "I hate to ask this, but can you walk across the sand in those shoes?"

"Why do you hate to ask that?"

He lowered his voice. "Because from the moment I saw you tonight, I've had this fantasy running through my head, and it involves you wearing those shoes."

"That's funny." She ran a hand down his chest, tracing over the ridges of his washboard abs. She couldn't get enough of his heat and sculpted lines. "I've had a fantasy running, too. Mine involves you wearing this shirt, only its buttons are scattered all over the bedroom floor."

Asher tilted his head skyward and growl-groaned toward the stars. "You're killing me, Brooke. Get them off."

She imagined him using that phrase back in the room. *Get them off, Brooke. Get those fucking panties off right now.*

How long had it been since a man had been so desperate to have her that he made such demands? Brooke shivered. Too long.

"Are you cold?"

"No." Brooke couldn't look at him. She was sure her thoughts were written all over her face, but they had to at least get through dinner. "I'm good."

Using Asher's forearm for balance, Brooke slipped out of the sandals. Asher took them from her and ushered her down the torch-lit path.

Once they were seated, a waiter appeared with a bottle of champagne.

"I'm not much for bubbly. Do you have any bourbon?" Asher asked.

"Of course, sir. Blanton's Gold is—"

"Hell, yeah," Asher interrupted. "That's perfect. I'd lost hope of finding a decent bottle on this island."

The waiter smiled, conspiratorially. "You haven't been looking in the right place. Would you like me to send a bottle to your room?"

"That would be great, thank you. I'm in Suite 8245."

He'd had all day to share that information with her and he hadn't. They hadn't traded cell numbers either.

Because this isn't a date and you aren't a couple. You're going to bang each other's brains out for a few days and then walk away. Just like last time.

She'd been hurt the last time. The sad truth was she'd take the hurt again to be with him, even for a few days. She was older and wiser than she'd been before. Heartache and pain wouldn't break her. The pain of being left behind *never* broke her.

"Very good, sir. Consider it done. For you, miss?" The waiter held the bottle of champagne for her to inspect.

"No, thank you. I had a sparkling mint and lime iced tea the other day. Can I get that here?"

"You don't want champagne?" Asher asked. "How about a glass of wine?"

"I'm not drinking tonight." She sent him a meaningful glance hidden behind a sweet-as-pie smile. "Stone-cold, I believe were the words you used."

"She'll take the tea," Asher told the waiter, his gaze never leaving hers. Once the man left to fetch their drinks, his lids lowered to slits. "I'm keeping track, starting now."

"Keeping track of what?"

"How many times you tempt me tonight. Remember —payback."

As much as she liked the sound of that, she wanted them both to be able to enjoy the meal. Technically, she was working. It wouldn't do her much good if she lost all the details in an Asher-induced lust-filled haze.

"All right. You win. I'll behave."

"You behaving is not a win for me, baby."

The waiter returned with their drinks. Another waiter immediately delivered a tray piled with cold shrimp and cubed lobster tails, along with small ramekins of clarified butter and a variety of other sauces for the shrimp.

They hadn't been given a menu, but it was kind of exciting, being served like royalty.

Small plates were placed in front of them and they dug in.

"Have you given any more thought to what you might do when your contract expires?"

Asher hesitated in the process of chewing a piece of shrimp. She watched as he swallowed then washed the food down with bourbon. The man even made eating sexy.

"Things are a little crazy right now. Lots of guys are getting out, retiring. It's hard to see my brothers being so content and happy without thinking about what-ifs for myself."

He stabbed a piece of lobster and dunked it in the butter.

"The thing is, being a SEAL is the only thing I know how to do, and I love my job. But sometimes I wonder..." He shook his head as if to erase whatever he was about to say. He brought the seafood to his lips, but spoke before it disappeared into his mouth. "It doesn't matter. I'll probably re-up."

An overwhelming sadness made it hard for Brooke to breathe. She knew what renewing his contract meant for Asher. It meant more one-night-stands, coming home to an empty apartment, never having love in his life. All because the stubborn ass couldn't see any other way.

His words also confirmed that these next few days were all she would have with him, so she'd better make them count.

"You have to follow your heart. If being a SEAL is what you love, then that's what you should do." And because she suspected what he'd been wondering about, she added, "You shouldn't have to sacrifice having a life outside the military, Ash. Any woman worthy of a man like you would never ask you to quit. She would be proud of the man you are and not try to change you."

"My mom is getting married. That's what this whole trip was about, although I didn't know until last night. She tricked me into taking leave, knowing I wouldn't want them traveling alone, because she couldn't imagine getting married without her kids by her side. Those were her words, by the way. Not mine."

Startled by the abrupt change in topic, Brooke floundered. "W-what?"

Asher dropped his fork on the table and sat back. "My mom is getting married. Here. This weekend."

A wedding? On the island? In a few days?

Brooke's creative brain took over her rational one. Using original—not stock—photos for the pitch would go a long way to completing her vision for the new campaign. It would add a personal touch she thought Gregory would appreciate. She would need to get permission from Asher's mom, which meant interacting with the woman. It also meant attending the wedding, which felt awkward and manipulative considering Asher hadn't invited her. She'd definitely need to discuss her thoughts with him first.

"That's exciting news." Although his expression said otherwise. "Do you get along well with the man she's marrying?"

Brooke knew from experience that wasn't always the case. The first guy her mom married after her dad left had been a total dick. The second guy had been a little better, but not much. The third guy Brooke had actually liked, and he seemed to like her as well. Brooke secretly believed that was the reason her mom kicked him out. Her mom didn't like sharing attention, even with her daughter.

She hoped Asher's situation was different.

"I get along with him fine."

"But, you're still not happy."

"He's my commanding officer."

"Oh." She was beginning to see why he wasn't more excited. If he didn't believe he could have a relationship because of his job, he would definitely feel the same way about his commanding officer.

"Yeah. Oh."

His gaze darted with obvious annoyance to the waiter who came to deliver their meal. Asher sat back, and Brooke did the same, giving the waiter room to remove their appetizer plates and replace them with dinner.

She and Asher both declined needing anything further and the waiter disappeared into the night.

Brooke stared at the plate. The perfectly seared steak, scallops, and green beans made her mouth water, but she didn't make any attempt to reach for the steak knife.

This conversation could go one of two ways. She could get onboard his unhappy train and commiserate, or she could dig deeper and potentially spoil the rest of their evening.

She never was much for commiserating.

"Are you upset that she's getting married, or that she's marrying another military man?"

The hard set of his mouth told her she'd nailed it. "He's not the right man for her."

"Sounds like your mom disagrees."

"Do you remember what we talked about the other night?" He stabbed his fork into the steak with more force than necessary, since she was sure the meat was tender enough to melt on her tongue.

To confirm, Brooke followed suit. As expected, her steak cut as easily as a hot knife through butter. "I remember your rant about SEALs and relationships. Or the impossibility of having a successful one."

She slipped a piece of steak into her mouth and had to bite back a groan at the delicious, smoky flavor.

Asher stopped in the process of making another slice and raised the tip of the knife to point at her. "Don't do that. Don't discount how I feel about the situation. Don't pretend you know anything about it. You don't know what it's like."

The sharpness in his tone pierced her chest. She methodically set her silverware on the table, her appetite waning as her temper flared to life.

"You don't think I know about loss? About how it feels to be left behind?" Damn it. Her eyes started to burn, a surefire signal that tears were on the way.

Her life wasn't so bad. She had ups and downs like everyone else. She'd had some losses, sure. But she'd also had some wins. She would not cry over things she couldn't change. Would *not*.

She smoothed the cloth napkin that covered her lap,

giving herself a minute to prepare before she opened old wounds.

"Brooke," Asher reached for her hand and Brooke jerked it back. If he touched her now she'd fall apart. He cursed softly. "I didn't mean to—"

"My dad left when I was nine, Asher. *Nine.*" When she met his gaze, he leaned back as if stunned at what he saw there. She didn't care. Let him see the pain he thought she didn't understand.

"I haven't seen or heard from him since. He might not have died a hero-in-battle as your father did. Hell, he might be alive and well for all I know. But, to me, he's as gone as your father. Then there's my mom..." She didn't have time to even begin that story. "Let's just say my mom lived her own life without any regard for her young daughter. Oh, did I forget to mention the fact that I was adopted? Which means my birth parents left me, too. And before you say something else idiotic about me *pretending* to know what it's like, let me remind you that I do have firsthand knowledge about how it feels to lose a man to the military. I lost *you.*"

Brooke crumpled the napkin in her lap, gathering it in her hand. She stood and dropped the napkin on the table, aware Asher was watching her every move.

She couldn't sit there and pretend her opinion of him hadn't been altered. She thought he was strong and solid, when in fact, he was nothing more than a coward. Too afraid to put himself out there for fear of getting hurt. It was one thing for him to sabotage his own life, but to want the same fate for the mother who loved him? Asher was right about one thing. She most definitely didn't understand *that.*

Brooke sensed the tears she could no longer hold back. She had ruined their dinner by not agreeing with him. While she was sorry for the dinner, she wasn't sorry for the other. His mom deserved his support. He was a jerk for not having her back.

"I don't regret one second of the time we spent together all those years ago," she admitted softly. "We can say it was all about sex, but we both know it was more than that. I've often wondered if the reason you didn't call was because you'd started to feel something for me."

"Jesus. Brooke. I—"

"No, let me get this out. Being with you was worth the hurt that came later. For a brief moment in time, you made me happy. You made my life a better place. It seems that remains true, because here I am, armed with the knowledge that nothing has changed, that there will never be a future for us, and wanting you anyway." She took a deep breath and brought her point home. "Maybe your mom believes her life was worth the pain, too."

She walked away then, leaving a stunned, speechless Asher to figure out the rest on his own. He would come after her, she had no doubt. What she didn't know was where they went from there.

She couldn't deny anymore that she loved him. She'd *always* loved him. It made sense, considering her track record. She'd been going through the motions, subconsciously waiting for a man she could never have.

He'd chosen the Navy over her, without realizing he could have both. Could still have both, if he ever got his head out of his ass.

Brooke didn't take the torch-lit path back to the golf cart. She headed down the beach. Other than herself, Asher, and a couple of waiters, the beach was deserted. She assumed that was because this side of the resort wasn't open to the public yet, but she'd seen people on this section of beach during the day.

Brooke wandered toward the edge of the water. She sat down where the waves would just reach her toes and hugged her knees to her chest. She stared out at the ocean, finally letting the soft stream of tears have their way.

She didn't know how long she sat there before she sensed she wasn't alone. A soft rustling of footsteps on the sand was further proof.

Tears long dried, Brooke stood and straightened her skirt, brushing off the sand she could reach, not caring about the sand she couldn't.

Not knowing what kind of mood Asher would be in, she steeled herself for the worst. When she turned around, the worst was what she found.

Brett, along with four of his friends she recognized from Cavalier's, were fanned out around her.

"Well, well, well," Brett said, his nasty grin slow to spread as he took a step toward her. "What have we here?"

10

————

ASHER REMEMBERED A TIME DURING BUD/S when he'd been in the freezing-cold waters of the ocean for so long, his mind had detached from his body. Nothing worked properly. Not his limbs. Not his lungs. Nothing.

That was exactly how he felt as he watched Brooke walk away.

He wanted to reach out, call to her, anything to get her to stay, *stay*, but her words had rendered him useless.

I lost you. Maybe your mom believes her life was worth the pain, too.

Is that what his mom believed? He didn't know, because they never talked about his dad. Now, more than ever, Asher knew the convo with his mom needed to happen, sooner rather than later. But first, he needed to focus on making his legs work so he could go find Brooke.

God, the way she'd looked at him before she walked away gutted him. As though she'd peeled back his layers and didn't like what she found. He'd never forget how heart-broken and fragile she looked, even as she was putting him in his place. His little firecracker.

His.

He didn't know how to make things right between them, but he sure as shit wouldn't figure it out sitting on his ass like a moron.

Asher pushed away from the table and stood, relieved that his legs supported his weight. He wiped his mouth with the napkin, then tossed it on the table. Not wanting to trek down the sand in his dress shoes, he kicked them off. His heart clenched as he set them on the sand next to Brooke's. She was out there, alone, without her shoes.

Asher ducked under the rim of the canopy. It took his eyes a minute to adjust to the dimness of the night. From his higher elevation he could see the stretch of beach below. Off to the right, he noticed a shadowy group of people in the distance. They were walking toward the water. Normally, Asher wouldn't think twice about people walking on the beach at night, but Brooke was out there and something in his gut turned over, his instincts screaming *trouble.*

He broke into a jog, keeping his eye on the group while frantically searching for any sign of Brooke. There. A slim figure sitting close to the water. *Brooke.* It seemed the group had seen her as well, because they were headed right for her.

Staying low, Asher slowed and focused on the group. With only the moonlight to help, he studied the shadows. There were four of them. They walked with the distinct gate of younger men who weren't as cool as they thought they were.

Asher cursed. He had a pretty good idea who the men were, and if he was right, he wanted backup. Not to help him kick their asses, but to haul off their carcasses once he was finished.

Asher pulled out his cell phone as he moved quietly

across the dunes of sand, heading for the beach below. He called the last person he wanted to talk to right now, but the only guy who could help.

"Asher?"

Asher stumbled over his own feet at the commander's use of his given name. The guy had never called him Asher before. Only used his rank. Something akin to affection warmed Asher's chest.

"Sir," Asher said in a hushed tone. So far the men had been too focused on their target to notice him, but the longer he could keep his presence unknown, the better. "There's about to be a potentially sticky situation on the beach. Could you grab hotel security and bring them down here, ASAP."

"What's the situation?" He could hear the commander shuffling around. The guy was already on the move. The warming thing going on in Asher's chest spread out, filling tiny cracks inside him that he hadn't known existed.

The late night pizzas, the advice, the encouragement throughout his career. This man had always had his back. Not as a superior officer, but as a ... a father.

The realization hit him like a Mack truck going ninety, but his concern for Brooke over-rode the crash.

"It's too dark. I'm too far away to know for sure, but I'm on the move. If I were to guess, it's some guys looking for payback for an incident involving a woman a few days ago." His gaze tracked to her. Brooke was still sitting, unaware she was being stalked.

Asher's throat ached from holding in her name. He wanted to call to her, but alerting her to the potential danger would also alert the group homing in on her. Four against one odds would go better if he had the element of surprise on his side.

Asher heard a door creak, followed by the distinct sounds of footfalls making short work of a stairwell.

"Would this happen to be the same woman your mother mentioned jumped from a moving boat yesterday?" The commander's voice echoed, accentuating his words with every step.

"Yes, sir." Asher felt an inexplicable pride, as if his affirmative somehow staked his claim. "One and the same."

"Is she with you?"

"She was." Heart pounding, eyes glued to Brooke, and still moving toward her, Asher gave a quick rundown. "We had an argument and she took off. I shouldn't have let her go alone, but I was giving us both time to cool off. I was on my way to find her when I noticed I wasn't the only one."

"How many?"

"Four, sir."

"Roger, that. Give me your location."

Asher rattled off an approximation. He had no doubt the commander would find him.

"I'm headed your way, and for God's sake, Lieutenant, don't kill any of them."

Asher snorted and hung up without giving any assurances. He was close now. Close enough to see Brooke stand and brush the sand from her backside. The men had fanned out, most likely to prevent her escape. Brooke turned and Asher heard her gasp drift through the air.

Don't worry, baby. I'm here. I've got you.

"Well, well, well. What have we here?"

As suspected, Asher recognized Brett's voice. Brett reached for Brooke and she stumbled back, her feet splashing through the water.

Asher sprang into action. He only had one shot at the element of surprise and he didn't waste it. He grabbed the guy closest to him from behind, wrapping his arm around his throat in a choke hold and dragging him backward. Within seconds the guy was out cold and Asher tossed him aside like a rag doll.

Out of the corner of his eye, he saw Brooke, her hands locking around Brett's wrists as the guy tried to grab hold.

Adrenaline pumping full steam now, Asher growled as the other two on the beach caught on and came for him. He threw out his arm at the last minute, clotheslining the first guy to reach him. The guy went down hard, clutching his throat.

Seeing two of his buddies on the ground, the third guy drew up. The guy held out his palms, as if that would stop Asher.

"I didn't touch her, man."

Asher raised his palms, mirroring the guy, but his feet never stopped moving. When he got close enough he did a fast pivot and with a surge of violent strength, slammed his fist into the guy's face. Before he could recover, Asher straight-armed the guy's chest, shoving him back. Asher hit him again, twice in rapid succession and the guy went down like a pump handle.

"Asher!"

Brooke's scream broke something open inside him. Hot, liquid heat filled his veins. Blood rushed through his ears and the world turned red.

Chest heaving, Asher spun toward the sound of her voice in time to see Brett tackle her on the hard sand. She landed on her stomach with Brett falling on top of her.

Asher took off toward them at a dead run, Brett's drunken laughter mixed with Brooke's cries as she struggled to get free. Brett reached for the zipper on the back of

Brooke's dress. Snarling, Asher lunged, hooking Brett around the waist and hauling him away from Brooke.

When they hit the ground, Asher shoved his feet into the sand, keeping Brett under him. Brett threw his elbow back, catching Asher in the jaw. Asher grabbed the guy's wrist and wrenched it up between his shoulder blades. With his other hand, he palmed the kid's skull and shoved his cheek hard against the sand. With the guy subdued, Asher shifted his body weight. He drove his knee into Brett's back and leaned down, putting his mouth close to the kid's ear.

His whole body vibrated with unspent rage. The piece of shit thought he could put his hands on Brooke?

"I warned you what would happen if you touched my girl again, motherfucker. Since I can't make you limp from this position, I'll have to find another way to make my point." Asher jerked the guy's arm higher.

Brett cried out. The guy reeked of smoke and alcohol. "No, no. Please, man. You're gonna break my arm!"

"Oh, *now* you realize the meaning of the word *no*? How about I teach you what it feels like when that word is ignored."

"Lieutenant!"

The commander's voice barely registered, Asher's sole focus on making the motherfucker under him *hurt*. Asher increased the pressure on Brett's arm. "I hope you're a lefty."

"Lieutenant! That's enough."

"Asher. Please. Let him go."

Brooke's voice was the only sound that had the strength to penetrate his anger. Asher's gaze snapped up. He searched, searched, and finally, he found her. She was close by, standing next to a man wearing a security uniform. Her dress was wrinkled and, for some reason, wet. Her hair was a mess, her cheeks tear-stained, her eyes puffy and red. She was the most beautiful woman he'd ever seen.

Brett shifted under him, apparently too high, drunk, and stupid to stay still. He tried to jerk his arm free. Before Asher could release him, a satisfying *snap* met his ears and Brett howled in pain.

Asher let go of Brett's arm, knowing the dislocated shoulder would hurt like a bitch when he did. He might've also used the guy's back as leverage to get to his feet.

"You all right?" the commander asked from somewhere on his left, but Asher only had eyes for Brooke.

"Fine." He took a step toward her. "Where are the other three?"

"We've got 'em."

Another step. Close enough to see her entire body trembled, and it flayed him wide open.

"Make sure they're escorted off this island, pronto. I need to..." Asher let his words die off as he walked away. For the first time in his life he didn't care about honor or duty or the fact that he'd just issued an order to his commanding officer.

The only thing he cared about was Brooke.

BROOKE HAD NEVER SEEN anything more violent in her life. Or more beautiful.

She managed to see most of the action while she evaded Brett's drunken, sloppy attempts to grab her. Watching Asher fight was like watching fluid art, every move sleek and efficient and utterly arousing. She'd been distracted long enough by the display to give Brett the upper hand.

A shuddered racked Brooke's body. She could still feel

Brett's weight on top of her. Could feel the cool night air against her backside, indicating her dress had ridden up enough to expose her panties.

The next thing she'd known, she was free. Like a wild predator, Asher charged in, latched onto his prey, and saved her from a horrible fate.

Asher had singlehandedly taken down four men. He'd broken a bone. For *her*.

"You've got to stop running away from me, sassy girl." He marched toward her, a man on a mission.

"You, first," she whispered, her throat raw and aching.

Asher's clothes were covered with sand. His knuckles looked red and angry. His jaw had started to swell on one side. But his eyes ... his eyes were shimmering bright with a mixture of sorrow, heat, and concern unlike any she'd seen before.

"I'm okay," she assured him. She was safe. He had come for her, as she'd known he would, because that's who he was. Whether he would admit it or not, he cared about her. She knew he did.

"I'm okay," she repeated as a sob broke through her lips. Seeing him there, whole and relatively unharmed, Brooke suddenly felt drained and weak. Her legs wobbled as though they were clocking out for the night. Before her knees could hit the sand, Asher was there, pulling her against him. His knees were the ones to hit the sand as she wrapped herself around him and buried her face against the side of his neck.

"Shh. Sweetheart. Don't cry." His warm, masculine scent filled her, calmed her, made everything seem all right again.

"I'm sorry, Brooke. I'm so sorry. Don't cry, sweetheart. I've got you." He murmured again and again, gently rocking them as he stroked his hand over her hair.

How could she, for even one moment, think this man wasn't solid? Misguided, maybe, but his heart was in the right place. She realized that now.

He loved his mom. He only wanted what was best for her, but his judgement was clouded by the past. And whose wasn't? She condemned Asher for shutting out the possibilities outside of the military, but hadn't she done the same thing with her own job? She'd sacrificed countless relationships because of her work and she couldn't even blame it on the money. She was on salary, so forty hours a week or eighty, her paycheck remained the same.

"Brooke." Asher's voice sounded strangled. He reached out, brushing his thumb across her cheek to catch her tears.

"I'm okay," she said for the third time, but this time, she meant it. Obviously, some things needed to change. She needed to take a long, hard look at her life and decide what she deemed truly important, without input from her inner nine-year-old.

As for Asher, he thought keeping her at arm's length was for her own good. Well, she was going to prove him wrong.

Brooke sniffed sharply, then wiped her eyes. "Can we get out of here?"

"Where do you want to go?"

"Somewhere I can shower off the sand." And maybe burn her dress. It was one of her favorites, but she doubted she'd ever get the smell of Brett's cologne out of the fabric. "My room, I guess."

He reached behind his head and gently pulled her hands from around his neck. Brooke shifted from his lap to the sand and Asher stood. She raised a hand, wanting him to pull her up, but instead, he bent down and scooped her back into his arms.

Legs dangling, Brooke looped her arm around his neck. "What are you doing?"

"You don't have any shoes." Asher started walking toward the canopy where their dinner sat, cold by now.

"Neither do you. You can put me down, you know."

He shook his head. "Can't. Not yet."

Brooke studied his chiseled profile. She ran a finger along his jawline, fascinated by the way the muscles tightened against her touch. "Are you okay?"

"Why do you ask?"

"You broke Brett's arm."

"He put his hands on you. And the arm will be fine ... eventually. The dumbass dislocated his own shoulder because he struggled when he should've played dead." The corner of Asher's mouth twitched. "If he thinks the pain is bad now, he's in for a real treat when the alcohol and dope wear off."

Brooke shouldn't have been happy about another person's suffering, but she couldn't conjure one ounce of sympathy for the guy.

Asher carried her to the golf cart, stopping only to ask one of the waiters to grab their shoes and Brooke's purse.

Asher set her down and slid onto the seat in the back of the cart. Since he didn't slide over to make room for her, Brooke turned to walk around to the other side.

"No. Don't." Asher stopped her with a hand on her wrist. He tugged her onto his lap, his arms once again circling her waist. "I need to ... just let me hold you."

The waiter delivered their belongings and then took the wheel.

Brooke relaxed against Asher's chest for the ride. Neither one of them spoke. When they got back to the hotel,

Asher took her hand and led her through the lobby toward a bank of elevators. Brooke pulled up short.

"We're going to your room? Are you sure that's a good idea? What about your mom and sister?"

Asher backed her into the empty elevator. "They have their own room. Your suite might be swankier than mine, but I've got a better view."

And boy he wasn't kidding. Brooke sucked in a breath as she crossed the threshold of Asher's suite. The living space was lined with windows. There was a door that lead to the balcony and she couldn't resist. Brooke ran to it, pulled it open, and stepped into the night. There was nothing but stars and ocean for as far as the eye could see. If she didn't look down toward the beach, she almost felt like she was flying.

"Pretty great, right?"

Brooke hummed her agreement as the heat from Asher's body warmed her back. Nerves struck her hard and fast, her belly erupting with fluttering butterflies. This was it. After eight long years, she would finally have him again. But, the question remained, would she be able to keep him?

The answer didn't matter tonight.

His fingers caressed the bare skin of her shoulders, traveled down her arms and back up again. A feather-light touch on the back of her neck made her shiver. She wrapped her hands around the top of the balcony railing as he traced the line of her dress, dipping down below her shoulder blades.

Her breath caught when he reached the top of her zipper. He hesitated.

"Don't think about him." His voice was heavy, gruff. "He doesn't get a say in what happens here. He doesn't get a say in what happens between us, ever."

Brooke realized then what Asher was doing. He was trying to replace Brett's touch with his own. She appreciated the gesture, but she had no trouble differentiating between his touch and Brett's.

She spun around, a hungry, needy sound ripping from her throat. She clutched his shoulders. "You're the only man I'm thinking about."

His arm came around her at the same time his mouth met hers, immediately taking the kiss from one to a thousand in the space of a heartbeat. He shoved a hand in her hair, tugging her head where he wanted it. It seemed Asher had no time for gentle and sweet, which suited her just fine. She had her own pent-up need to unleash.

"Gotta get inside you," Asher murmured against her lips. "Need to feel you around me."

"*Yes.*"

Asher deepened the kiss as Brooke felt her feet leave the ground. He devoured her. He worked her mouth with precision, a man who took what he wanted and made no apologies. His tongue was hot and determined, and oh, so wicked. She sucked him into her mouth and Asher groaned, tightening his hold on her.

The next thing Brooke knew, she was horizontal on the bed. Asher nudged her legs apart with his knee, and she opened for him, wanting his weight against her, pressing her into the mattress. He settled between her thighs. She rocked her hips, desperate to feel the hard ridge of his erection. She gasped against his mouth as she found him hot, hard, ready.

A wave of dizzying lust caught Brook off guard. She dug her nails into his shoulders, an anchor to keep her grounded.

Asher broke the kiss with a curse. He shoved back, the loss of his heat leaving her wanting. She was about to complain, but his fingers were already working the buttons on his shirt. Brooke rose to her elbows, riveted, her gaze glued to the skin he revealed, inch-by-inch. When he opened the button at his waistband, Asher switched gears and went to work on his belt.

He glanced up and caught her staring. "This show ain't free, baby. Tit for tat. It's your turn. Pull up your skirt. Show me where my cock is aching to be."

Her belly dipped as she sat up. She grabbed hold of the edge of her dress and slowly, so slowly, teased the material up her legs, stopping just before she revealed her panties.

Asher licked his lips, the heat in his gaze scorching her, making her feel brazen.

"Is this what you want to see?" She shimmied the material over the tops of her thighs. Brooke bit her lip as he pulled his belt free of his pants with a wide sweep of his arm. The buckle clanked softly as he tossed it away.

"Show me," he demanded. His pants were the next thing to hit the floor. He kicked them away and stood by the end of the bed in nothing but boxer briefs, waiting. His erection was thick and heavy, pressing against the material as if trying to reach for her. Brooke laid back, taking the hem of her dress with her, exposing her panties and belly.

"You'll need to unzip me if you want to see the rest."

A condom landed on the bed next to her as Asher put his hands on her knees and slowly trailed up her thighs. His thumbs traced the edge of her panties, but he didn't go where she needed him. He teased over her sex, avoiding her clit, as he continued to move up her body.

"Asher," she groaned.

"I want to see it all," he said as he slipped his hands under her. Brooke arched her back, giving him better access to the zipper. Within seconds, he had it open. He fisted the thick straps of the dress and yanked them down her arms, freeing her naked breasts.

"*Christ*, you're beautiful. You make me wonder how I've lived all these years without your perfect body underneath mine. Without your mouth. Without these."

Asher bent his head, taking a nipple into his mouth. He sucked hard and released her with a *pop*. "There are so many things I want to do right now." He plumped her other nipple between his fingers until she shook with the sensation. "But I can't wait, Brooke. I need you."

Brooke was beyond words. She nodded. *Yes, yes, yes.* He wasn't the only one desperate. She wanted him inside her more than she wanted her next breath. Her clit throbbed for attention. Her breast still held the warmth and sting from his mouth. She needed him. *Now.*

She wrestled her arms from the material of her dress as Asher moved back to strip off his briefs. She worked her panties down her legs and just like that, they were both naked.

Asher's gaze darkened as he wrapped a hand around his cock and stroked from base to tip. He was bigger than she remembered. Thick and heavily veined, the tip an angry red.

"I've had this exact dream," he told her. "You, naked and spread out on my bed, wet and ready for me." He dragged a finger over her slit. "I like the live version better."

So did she.

He reached for the condom, tore open the package, and rolled it down. Brooke scooted up the bed as he crawled over her like a predator stalking his prey. His elbow came to rest beside her head. With his other hand, he teased the head of his erection up and down her sex. Once, twice, and then he circled her opening and, without warning, shoved deep.

Asher dropped his forehead against her shoulder. "I want to go slow, Brooke, but *fuck me*, you feel good. So fucking hot and tight around me."

"Go slow next time," she panted. "For now, just *move*." In case he didn't realize she was serious, Brooke squeezed her inner muscles hard.

"You're gonna pay for that, sassy girl," Asher growled and pulled all the way out.

"Asher," she whimpered, the heat radiating from his head hovering right above her clit. She rolled her hips. If he would just—

"Say please."

"Please. God. Please!"

Those were the last words either one of them said for a while. Their mouths met in a tangle of tongues and scorching heat as Asher rammed his cock into her, the force of it moving them up the bed.

She was close, and he'd barely gotten started. He stretched her with every pump of his hips, touched her deep, in a place no other man had reached.

Brooke broke away from his mouth. She arched up to meet his thrusts, the force of his hips driving the breath from her lungs. The tingling started in her toes and shot all the way through her. Her thighs quivered.

"Open your eyes, baby," Asher said from above her. "Look at me. I want to see those pretty blues as you come."

Brooke hadn't even realized her eyes were closed. She found his gaze and held there, drowning in a rich pool of emotion at being with him again, like this. Joined together, as close as two people could be.

His jaw was clenched tight and she knew he was holding out for her.

She slipped her hand between them, brushing her clit with the pad of her finger. That was all it took. The orgasm hit her fast and hard, locking her muscles down tight. The pleasure was almost too much to bear as Asher kept working her, pumping his hips faster as her sex continued to clench around him.

"*Fuck,*" Asher groaned. "That's it. Jesus. You feel so good."

He drove into her once more and stilled, his chest heaving as he came, pulsing inside her.

He dropped his forehead to hers, their pants mingling in the sliver of space between their lips. Brooke caressed his sweat-dampened back, soothing them both now that the storm had passed.

"Stay with me tonight. I'm not ready to let you go."

You don't have to. Not ever.

"I'm not going anywhere."

11

———

Bang, *bang*, *bang*, *bang!*

Asher rolled over and let out a long-suffering groan. *Not again.* He knew damn well if he didn't get up and answer the door, his sister would continue to pound on it until he did.

Bang, bang, bang, bang!

Case in point.

Beside him, Brooke rolled over and stretched her limbs. She looked good in his bed. She'd look even better on his lap, riding his morning wood as he played with her perfect—

Bang, bang, bang, bang!

Brooke sat up, clutching the sheet to her chest. "What is that? Is someone here?"

"*That* is my lovely, soon-to-be-strangled sister." Panic flashed through Brooke's eyes and he glared at her. "Don't you dare move," he warned. "I'll get rid of her."

Asher rolled out of bed. He could feel Brooke's eyes on him as he rummaged around for a clean pair of pants. Just to be ornery, he grabbed the jeans. He tugged them on, grunting as his balls shifted and shoved against the denim

in protest. Commando and jeans? Not always the best decision. With a quick adjustment, he carefully zipped, but left
the button undone. He shoved his arms into a sleeveless
gray tee and pulled it over his head.

Bang, bang, bang, bang!

He yelled to Gracie to *hold her fucking horses*. He shot
Brooke a wicked grin, loving the way she licked her lips as
she looked him over.

He was so amped last night after the fight, after seeing
that motherfucker's hands on her. At first, he just wanted
her close, to reassure himself that she was okay. Unharmed
and safe. And then ... then he'd been all about getting inside
her. He needed to erase every bad thing that had happened
—the argument, Brooke walking away, finding Brett and his
assholes on the beach—and replace them with something
good. Something *explosive*.

"Are you okay?" He hadn't been gentle with her last
night. Not the first time. Not the second time, when she
woke him by rubbing her ass against his dick and he slid in,
taking her from behind. And not the third time, when
they'd finally made it to the shower.

"I'm naked in your bed, my dress isn't fit for public, and
Grace is at the door. What do you think?"

I think I love you.

Not that he could tell her. He tucked the words away
where they belonged—nowhere near this amazing woman
who deserved so much more than he could give her.

He stretched across the bed and kissed her. "Sounds
perfect to me. Minus the Gracie, part. I'll just go take care of
that right now."

"You better," she called as he left the bedroom, closing
the door behind him.

When he opened the door to the suite, Gracie was

PARKER KINCADE

leaning against the wall, inspecting her fingernails. She glanced up and straightened. "Took you long enough."

Asher held the door open with one arm and gripped the jamb with the other, blocking the doorway. "Nope. Not this morning. Take a hike, squirt."

"Why? Is Brooke here?" When he didn't answer, she blew out a breath. "I'm here to warn you. Mom and Joel aren't far behind me. He told Mom and me what happened on the beach last night. Nice bruise, by the way." She poked at his jaw.

"Hey, knock it off." Asher jerked his head back and slapped her hand away, his irritation mounting. "What do you mean they're right behind you?"

"I mean, you've got about ten minutes before the firing squad commences. With food. They're bringing breakfast. And questions. Mom's worried."

With that, Gracie spun on her heel. Asher leaned out, watching until she got to the door to her room. She gave him one last look, stuck her tongue out, then disappeared inside.

Asher shut the door. He leaned his back against it and banged his head against the smooth wood a couple of times. What the hell was he going to do now?

Asking Brooke to leave felt all kinds of wrong, but they'd been down this road before and it hadn't ended well for him. He knew this time wouldn't be any different. Might even be worse, since it would be obvious to everyone what he and Brooke had been doing last night.

He pushed away from the door.

You know what? Fuck it. He was making too big a deal. They were all adults. It wasn't as if Brooke hadn't met his mom before, and she'd been sitting with Gracie yesterday— a fact he'd meant to ask her about but forgot.

He and Brooke could share a meal with his family without it being a life-altering event.

When Asher walked back into the bedroom, Brooke was spread out on his bed like a fucking Sunday buffet. Her arms were thrown over her head, giving him a pretty good idea of how she would look restrained. Her breasts were high and tight, the pretty pink tips peaked. Her rib cage moved in smooth waves with each breath. Her stomach was firm and flat.

Asher's gaze trailed lower, where the sheet covered the rest of her. But he knew what was underneath. A sweet pussy and legs that should be wrapped around his head right now as he buried his face beneath a strip of golden curls.

"You done?" she asked.

God, he loved that sassy mouth. He glanced around. "This isn't my patio, but I warned you I'd do more than look if you showed up topless."

He watched, entranced, as Brooke palmed her breasts, pushing the beautiful mounds together while her legs scissored under the sheet.

Ten minutes. You've got ten minutes.

He only needed five.

It occurred to him as he jerked the sheet from her body that he should warn her, give her time to dress and get out of there if that's what she wanted to do. But then his gaze found hers, and he saw the longing there. Being the greedy bastard he was, he did the only thing he could do. He grabbed her ankles.

Brooke squeaked as he jerked her down the bed. He went to his knees, used his shoulders to shove her thighs wide, and took the taste he'd been aching for.

Brooke Ramsey was more delicious than the best

bourbon in the world. She was one hundred and ninety proof of smoky-sweet woman.

Firming his tongue, Asher licked up her center, capturing her wet heat and drinking it down. He wanted to savor her, to memorize every sound and move she made as she ground her pussy against his face.

Damn the god of time for always working against him.

Using his thumbs, Asher spread her open. He dipped low, teasing the tiny rosebud between her cheeks with the tip of his tongue. Yeah, she liked that. His girl didn't mind getting a little dirty. She moaned his name, her fingers diving into his hair and hanging on.

He circled her again, then got down to business, finding her tight, swollen clit and curling his tongue around it. He took his cues from her, finding the rhythm she needed to fly. He worked her, without mercy.

He pressed a palm to her stomach. Her muscles were tight, ready to contract and give him what he wanted. He teased around her opening with his fingers. She was so wet, he easily slid two of them inside.

"I'm close, Ash. *Please.* Don't stop."

Never.

He curled the fingers inside her, hitting her in just the right spot as he flicked her clit with his tongue. She came apart, screaming his name the way he wanted her to for the rest of his fucking life.

He knew from the moment he saw her again that he was in serious trouble with this girl. Every day that passed he fell deeper and deeper. And any minute now his mom would knock on the door, bringing with her the reality of his situation.

He wanted Brooke, but he didn't know how to keep her.

Not without hurting her. And after what he'd learned about her life last night, she'd been hurt enough.

He placed a soft kiss against her mound and stood, staring down at her. Well and thoroughly pleasured looked good on her. He hated to ruin the moment.

"Come on, sweetheart. As much as I like you tangled in my sheets, it's time to get out of bed."

Brooke pushed up on her hands as he headed for the bathroom. He went to the sink and turned on the water. He leaned over and splashed his face, sadly removing all evidence of Brooke from his lips and chin.

He had just grabbed his toothbrush when Brooke came in, naked and glorious, and god, he loved that she didn't try to hide her body from him.

"I like the jeans, by the way." She grinned.

He'd wear them every goddamned day. "You need to get dressed."

"What's the rush?" She came to him, wrapped her arms around him from behind, and snuggled her face against his back. Asher caught her naughty little fingers as they slipped under his shirt to toy with the button on his jeans.

"Don't do that." He immediately regretted the harshness in his tone, but *fuck*. He was about to pop and having her naked little body tucked against him wasn't helping matters any.

She stiffened and took a step back. "Sorry."

He tried to brush it off. "Don't be sorry, baby. I just need you to get dressed. Please." He shoved the toothbrush in his mouth and went to work.

"If you want me to leave, just say so."

He spit toothpaste into the sink and rinsed his mouth. "I don't—" The knock on the door cut him off.

Brooke grabbed a towel and wrapped it around herself. "Are you expecting someone else?"

Asher stepped out of arm's reach, in case she decided to take a swing at him. "That would be my family. The commander told my mom what happened last night and she's concerned."

The color left her cheeks. "You knew they were coming and didn't tell me?"

Since he was already in the dog house, Asher decided not to give her any more reasons to keep him there. "To be clear, I don't want you to leave. There's an unopened toothbrush in the cabinet. Help yourself to whatever you need from my bag."

"Asher."

He backed his way out of the room. "Better hurry up and get dressed, sassy girl. You don't want your breakfast to get cold."

BROOKE DID the best she could with what she had to work with. She'd fallen asleep last night with wet hair, so this morning it was a curly mess. One swipe of a brush and it would become a *frizzy* mess. She dug around in her purse and found a stray hair band. She finger-combed the worst of the curls. She secured the tresses in a low ponytail, leaving a few golden wisps around her face.

She found the toothbrush Asher mentioned. Using the toothpaste he left on the counter she was able to scrub her mouth clean. She washed her face. She could use some mascara, but the natural look would have to do.

Her dress was another matter. The material was horribly wrinkled from being on the floor all night. The lower part of the skirt was stained with salt-water, and there were smudge marks along the front. She did her best to wipe those away with a damp towel, and then she used a hairdryer to dry the spots.

Brooke would've appreciated the opportunity to make a better second impression, since her first had been an epic fail, her jumping off the back of a boat and all.

There was nothing she could do about it now. She wouldn't have a hope in hell of convincing Asher that they belonged together if she couldn't even face his family in less than stellar condition.

She could do this.

Squaring her shoulders, Brooke left the safety of the bedroom.

"Brooke!" Grace bounced over and wrapped her skinny arms around Brooke's waist, hugging her like a long-lost friend instead of a woman she'd only known for five minutes.

"Oh. Um." Stunned laughter fell from her mouth as Brooke patted the girl's back. "Hey, Gracie."

Grace reared back.

"What?" Oh god. Had she messed up already?

"You called me Gracie. Only Joel and Asher call me that."

Had she? Shit. She'd heard Asher use the name and it just slipped out. "I'm sorry, I didn't mean—"

Grace beamed. "I like it. Come on."

Brooke was helpless against Grace's bubbly excitement, so she allowed herself to be dragged deeper into the room.

"Joel found these really great pastries," Grace said as they reached the dining area. "You've gotta try one."

Asher came to the rescue. "Okay, Gracie. Give Brooke a minute to catch her breath." He slipped an arm around her and pressed a quick kiss against the side of her head. "You're always so beautiful," he whispered for her ears alone. "You and Gracie seem chummy. Remind me later to get the story of how that came about."

Before she could respond, Asher's mom was there. Shorter than Brooke by several inches, Brooke had to bend down when Ellen tugged her away from Asher and wrapped her in a hard and fast hug.

"Are you okay?" Ellen asked. "Joel told us about last night. Come, sit."

Good lord. Brooke had been hugged more in the last five minutes than in the last five years, that was for sure.

A man she recognized from last night on the beach stood. "I'm sorry we didn't get the chance to be properly introduced last night. I'm Joel Taylor."

Brooke had surmised who he was before he even spoke. She shook his proffered hand. "It's nice to meet you, Commander Taylor. Thank you for your help."

Something akin to approval shone in his eyes. "Please, there's no need for formality here. Call me Joel. I'm just glad you're all right." He turned his attention to Asher. "And what about you? How's that jaw this morning?"

Asher guided Brooke into a chair. He slid into the one next to her. "Gracie hits harder than that jackass on the beach." No one even raised a brow at his language. "Where are they now?"

"I decided the best thing to do was get them off the island," Joel said. "They're on a plane back to Florida right now. But, don't worry. I made a few calls. Technically, they are all twenty-one, but they all have parents who are paying for their school. I called their fathers."

"You talked to all of them?"

"Every fucking one."

"Joel. Grace," Ellen hissed softly.

"I know the f-word, Mom!" Gracie called from her place on the couch. She was stretched out on her stomach, flipping through a magazine. "Asher says it all the time, too."

"Hey, thanks for tossing me under the bus, squirt."

"Like Mom doesn't already know how you Navy boys are." Grace snorted and flipped a page. "Please."

Brooke was fascinated. They joked and chastised, but the love and affection between the members of Asher's family were evident. And a little overwhelming.

Joel brought Ellen's knuckles to his lips and he kissed them softly. "I also spoke to the dean of their college, the head of their fraternity, and their coach. One thing is certain, there are at least four college football players who'll be riding the bench for the better part of next season, if not all. Not to mention facing probation and potential loss of scholarships. They won't soon forget the mistake they made."

Asher nudged her shoulder. "He doesn't mess around."

"Damn right I don't," Joel said. "Not when it comes to this family."

She wanted this in her life. She wanted people who would love her through thick and thin. People she could love and ... depend on to have her back. She didn't know how she'd fit in, not having any experience and all, but hey, she was the master at figuring shit out.

"They should get kicked out of school for behavior like that," Ellen declared. "And good riddance. I'm just glad they're gone and Brooke and Asher are okay."

Ellen got up and grabbed a tray of delicious-looking pastries and set it on the table, followed by a tray filled with fruit. "Don't be shy, Brooke. Grace, come get something to eat. We have a lot to do today."

Brooke put a Danish and some pineapple slices on her plate. "That's right. Asher tells me the two of you are getting married in a couple of days. Congratulations. That's exciting." Next to her, she felt Asher stiffen.

Ellen sat down and Joel dropped his arm over the back of her chair. They looked at each other with such warmth and affection that it made Brooke's chest ache. How could Asher not see how happy they were?

"Thank you, Brooke." Ellen smiled up at Joel. "We are very happy. I still can't believe it sometimes. We are in this beautiful place. The kids are here." Ellen's eyes filled with tears. "It couldn't be more perfect."

Grace bounced over. "Are you coming to the wedding?" She reached over Joel's shoulder and snatched a muffin off the tray.

Awkward.

"I—" Crap. She'd wanted to talk to Asher about it first.

"Oh, you must!" Ellen clapped her hands together. "It won't be a big to-do. Just us and a handful of friends and family who wanted to make the trip. You're more than welcome. Right, Ash?"

Casual as can be, Asher slipped his hand under the table.

"Of course she's welcome." His knuckles brushed the outside of her thigh, making her jump. The way they were positioned, Brooke knew no one could see, but he wouldn't dare. Would he? No. Not with his mom and Joel sitting across the table from them. Brooke held perfectly still, chewing on her bottom lip as his fingertips teased across her leg to her inner thigh, going higher, higher, higher. "I'd love for her to come."

Brooke grabbed hold of his wrist, stopping him just short of her panties. Naughty man.

"I'd love to come as well," she said, feeling Asher's fingers flex against her skin. "In fact, I wanted to talk to you both about an idea I had."

Ellen and Joel exchanged a glance. "We're all ears," Ellen said.

Brooke held Asher's wrist while she explained the reason she was at the resort, and then she outlined her idea for the ad campaign.

"So you see, with your permission, I'd like to take photographs during your wedding to potentially use for advertising the new resort. I'm not a professional photographer, of course, but I do have a nice camera that I bought specifically for this trip. I'd be happy to give you copies of all the pictures. If the resort likes what I put together, I'll have to get you to sign a release giving us permission to use the photos, but we don't have to worry about that right now. Also, if we use the photos, you'll be paid a standard fee. It's not much, but just so you know."

"What do you think, Joel?"

"I don't see the harm in it. Sure," Joel said. "Why not? Let's do it."

"Really? That's so great, thank you." Brooke couldn't contain her smile.

Asher leaned over and put his mouth against her ear. "The resort is gonna love your ideas, sweetheart. I have a few ideas of my own to share with you."

"About my campaign?"

"About how we're gonna break in that new camera of yours."

12

ASHER STOOD outside the door to his mom's suite. The week had slipped away from him. The wedding was tomorrow and he still hadn't had a moment alone with her.

Six days ago he'd been so sure his mom was making a mistake in marrying Commander Taylor. Now all he could think about were the words Brooke had said to him that night on the beach.

Brooke. Sexy, smart, creative, fun Brooke. After only a handful of days, he couldn't imagine how he would go back to a life without her.

He'd figured out a couple of things over the last few days. He loved Brooke, with everything that he was, and he was a Navy SEAL, through and through. Being a SEAL was in his blood. He wasn't ready to leave the military.

Which left him at odds.

If someone had asked him a week ago, he would've stood flat-footed and defended the choices he'd made. He hadn't subscribed to the bachelor life because he was against love and marriage—for other people. He'd done it because ... fuck. He didn't know anymore. He just knew he didn't ever want to be the source of Brooke's pain. If he kept his job, that was a definite possibility, no matter how hard he tried to make her happy.

Was it really possible for them to make a go of it? Did he have a chance in hell of keeping both Brooke *and* his job?

It was time to get some answers.

Asher knocked on the door. When his mom opened it, he didn't beat around the bush. "We need to talk."

"Sure. Come on in."

"Is Gracie here?"

"No. She and Joel are down on the beach. They should be back in a couple of hours. Where's Brooke?"

It still surprised him how easily his family accepted Brooke as a part of his life. They hadn't questioned him about how and where he had met her. Hadn't questioned the incredible coincidence of her being on the island at the exact same time. They embraced Brooke with open arms, as if she'd been there all along.

"She's getting things ready for the pitch meeting on Monday. Thought I'd give her some space."

His mom sat down on one end of the couch. "You two have spent a lot of time together this week."

Every day—sometimes just the two of them, sometimes doing things with his mom, Joel, and Gracie. And every night they crawled into bed, hungry and ready for each other. He never slept so soundly than when Brooke was spooned against him.

Asher took the other end of the couch, angling his body to face his mom. He stretched his arm along the top of the cushions. "We've had a lot of fun exploring the islands. She's taken some amazing photographs to use for her campaign. She really run with the whole 'couples experience' thing. I've seen some of what she's come up with. If I were in the market for a romantic getaway and saw her ads, I'd be sold. She's very creative."

"You seem happy with her. Does this mean we'll see more of her once we get home?"

"I don't know. I mean, yeah, that's what I want, but..."

"But, what?"

"I don't want to hurt her."

"Then, don't."

Asher rolled his eyes. "It's not that simple. You, of all people, should know that."

"No relationship is easy all the time, Ash. There is a reason the marriage vows include the words 'for better or for worse.' That doesn't mean you shouldn't try."

"You tried, and look where it got you. And you're about to willingly do it again. I don't get it, Mom. After everything you went through, I wouldn't think you'd be so quick to jump back into military life."

She looked at him then in the way she used to whenever he pissed her off, which had been quite often throughout his teen years. Her eyes narrowed. She squeezed her lips together and tilted her head as if trying to Jedi-mind-trick her way into his skull. When that didn't work, she started with the slow nod. Up, down. Up, down. Up, down.

He knew from experience if he tried to talk she'd only cut him off, so he waited her out. After about a minute of lip squeezing and head nodding, she finally spoke.

"I wouldn't call ten-plus years quick to jump, so let's just get that out of the way right now. Joel is a good and honorable man, as you well know. He loves me. He loves Grace. And whether you want to believe it or not, he loves you. He considers you the son he never had, although I'm certain he's never told you outright."

No, but looking back, Asher realized the commander

had done plenty to show him. And what had he done to show how much he appreciated Commander Taylor's presence and support over the years? He'd been a total dick the night they announced their wedding plans.

His mood sank.

"Do you regret marrying Dad?"

His mom's eyes flared wide with disbelief. "How could you ever think that?"

"How could I not? I was there, Mom. I remember the arguments and the hurt in your eyes whenever Dad had to bug out. I remember how sad you were that he missed the better part of your pregnancy with Gracie. I remember a lot more than that, too. And obviously, you were a mess when he died. You stayed in your room, crying for hours at a time. You were barely functional. You were such a mess that you didn't even make it to the funeral." It had been Commander Taylor—Joel—who had stood by Asher's side that day. "You walked around like a zombie for years after."

"Does this have anything to do with Brooke?" Tears filled his mom's eyes and he felt it deep in his gut.

"I don't ever want to make her feel the way you felt."

"Oh, Asher. I'm so sorry. I didn't realize you felt that way. You've got it all wrong, son."

"Jesus, Mom. Don't cry. You don't have anything to be sorry for. This isn't about Brooke," he lied. "I'm just trying to understand why you would put yourself in this position again."

"Would you be asking me this question if Joel weren't in the Navy?"

"Doubt it. At least a civilian man could give you the life you deserve." He was starting to sound like a broken record, and he hated it. "Do you regret being with Dad? I need to know."

"Asher." She drew in a deep breath. "There were things about my relationship with your dad that you don't understand."

"Then explain it to me. I'm not a kid anymore, Mom. I can handle whatever it is you have to say." Although if she confirmed his fears about moving forward with Brooke, he might have to hit something.

"You have to give me your word that you'll keep what I tell you to yourself. Joel, obviously, knows everything because he was your dad's best friend. But, there's no need to upset Grace. If she ever wants to know about her dad, I will be the one to tell her, got it?"

His heart kicked into overdrive. He felt sick. "Yeah, sure. You have my word."

"All right. Then, before I get into the nitty gritty, you need to know your father loved you more than anything. He was so proud to have a son. I don't want you to forget that."

Asher nodded. "I won't."

"I know some of this might be hard for you to understand, because he was careful to keep the ugliest parts of himself away from you." Her eyes took on a faraway look. "I loved your father very much. And he loved me, too, I think. At least in the beginning."

Oh yeah. He was definitely going to be sick.

"We were young. I was only eighteen when I had you. Your dad was twenty. Things were really good those first few years. He was settling into the Navy and working hard to make it into BUD/S training. I was settling into married life and being a mom.

"You were ... around seven, I think, when your dad started drinking. He wasn't a violent drunk, thank God, or things might've turned out very differently for us. A few years after that he had his first affair."

Jesus Christ. Asher closed his eyes, trying to reconcile the man he remembered with the one she described. "How did you find out?"

"Joel," she said quietly. "He confronted your dad. Actually, Joel kicked his ass. Told him if he didn't stop seeing the woman, Joel would tell me." She waved a hand. "The details don't matter. What matters is your father came home and told me about the other woman, and that Joel said he'd better do right by me. He apologized. Promised never to do it again. Turns out, he lied."

"He had more affairs? Why did you stay with him?"

Her smile was self-deprecating. "I loved him. I was young and inexperienced. Your dad was my first serious relationship. And I believed we could make it work."

"I still don't understand. You had Gracie."

"Asher Michael Dillon, you get that look off your face right now. I'm not the one who cheated. Your father is also Grace's father. He returned from an extended deployment the year before you turned fifteen, remember?"

Asher nodded, unable to form words.

"He came home and wanted to try again to be a good husband and father. I don't guess I need to explain to you how that reunion went since nine months later I had Grace. Things were good for a few weeks. Really good. And then word came down that he was being sent overseas. He didn't come home that night. Or the night after that." She stared down at her hands. "I called Joel," she said softly. "He went out and looked for him. Found him with yet another woman. Joel dragged him out of there and brought him home." A tear escaped her eyelid and she swiped it away. "Thank goodness you were staying at a friend's house that night, because we ended up having the worst fight in the history of our marriage. Joel actually stayed the night, refusing to leave me alone in the house with your father, even though he'd never been physically violent with me. They both shipped out the next afternoon. I never heard from your dad again."

They were both quiet for a few minutes, lost in the memories.

His mother cleared her throat. "As for what you remember? I hope you now understand the arguments and why I was hurt when your father left. I never knew if he was working or going to see another woman. It was maddening at times. Yes, I was devastated when your dad died. I was overly emotional with pregnancy hormones. The doctor warned me that my stress was putting Grace at risk. When Joel heard that, he refused to let me leave the house, even for the funeral. He thought I'd lost enough to your father; he didn't want me to risk losing Grace, too. Thank goodness she came less than a month later—which is why I was, I believe you said—walking around like a zombie for years after. I was sleep deprived from raising an infant and a teenaged son on my own. I struggled with postpartum depression for a time, and Joel was the one who helped me through it. He helped me through a lot of things."

She reached for a tissue and wiped her nose. "If I have a regret, it's that the last words your dad and I shared were in anger. So, to answer your question, no. I don't regret marrying your dad. Not at all. He gave me you and Grace, and I love you both with all my heart. And he brought me to Joel. I wouldn't trade one minute of my life with your father, no matter how painful it was at times, because those minutes got me here."

Asher scrubbed a hand over his face. This whole conversation was fucking with his head. It was like he was a stranger in his own life.

"But, his job." *My job.* Yeah, that whole argument was losing its steam.

"Our marital problems had nothing to do with your dad being in the Navy. I loved being a military wife. I loved being a part of something bigger than myself. Something important. Some of my best friends are military wives I met while your dad and I were married. Everyone has been very supportive of Joel and me. He's a good man, Asher."

"Yes, he is." More than Asher ever knew. "I'm happy for you, Mom. I hope you know I only want the best for you."

She reached out and touched his cheek. "And I want the best for you, too, son. So, make sure you don't do something stupid and let her get away."

13

——————

BROOKE STOOD in the doorway and watched as Asher shrugged into his tailored suit jacket. It had to be a custom job, the way the material hugged his wide shoulders and muscled arms. The suit was dark blue, almost black. He wore a crisp, white dress shirt and a solid colored tie that matched his suit to a T.

"You doing okay?" she asked.

Asher had been quiet all morning. In fact, he was quiet last night, too. He'd come to her suite late in the evening and, with barely a hello, had led her to bed, where he proceeded to make love to her until they both fell into an exhausted sleep.

"I'm fine." His smile was half-hearted. "Got a lot on my mind today, is all. You look gorgeous, as always."

She preened under his attention. She, Grace, and Ellen had combed the local shops to find Brooke the perfect dress for the wedding. The halter dress was a rich coral color that gave her skin the illusion of a deeper tan. The fabric was thin and flowing, the skirt made up of several layers to prevent any peekaboo. She'd taken extra time to curl her long hair into ringlets she let fall down her back, since she knew Asher preferred it that way. She wore a light coat of mascara, but no other makeup that she'd end up sweating off in the Caribbean sun.

"Thank you. Do you want to talk about whatever it is that's bothering you?"

"Not right now," he said, confirming he was indeed bothered by something. "Are you ready to go?"

The last few days he'd shown no signs of being upset about the wedding, so she thought he'd come to terms with it, if not gotten one hundred percent on board.

"Is it the wedding? Are you still—"

"I'm fine, but if we don't leave now I'm going to be late for the pictures and my mom will be pissed."

She tried and failed not to take his abrupt tone personally. He'd never spoken to her like that before, not eight years ago, not during the current week. It set alarm bells ringing in her head.

She moistened her lips, unsure how to feel about his attitude. "I need to grab my camera bag and then yes, I'm ready."

Asher collected her bag before she could and slipped the strap over his shoulder. He took her hand and they walked the short distance to the location where they were going to meet the professional photographer. Brooke stayed out of the way, snapping pictures of her own of the bride and groom from interesting angles she thought might work for the campaign. She would continue to take photographs throughout the afternoon and go through them all later that night to pick out the best ones.

She couldn't resist taking pictures of Asher, too. It should be illegal for a man to look as good in a suit as Asher did. She secretly couldn't wait until after the ceremony, when she knew he planned to shuck the tie and jacket. If she played her cards right, maybe he would let her help. She did so enjoy undressing him.

The ceremony didn't take long, but the couple had written vows that were so sweet, Brooke found herself dabbing at her eyes. Several times she caught Asher staring at her with an expression she couldn't begin to decipher. He didn't look angry, per say, but with his brows pinched and his back ramrod straight, he didn't look as happy as a best man should.

The afternoon got even more awkward when it came time to introduce her to Asher's few extended family members who had flown over to attend.

"This is Brooke," he'd say, time and time again. Not "my friend, Brooke." Not "my girlfriend, Brooke." Just, "this is Brooke," as though she wasn't important enough to have a title, a purpose in his life.

Hour by hour, she could feel him pulling away, and she didn't know why. By the time the festivities were winding down, Brooke was tense and exhausted from putting on a brave face.

"I think I'm going to head back to the room."

For the first time that day, Asher showed some concern for her. "Are you feeling okay?"

"Yes, just tired. Someone kept me up late last night," she teased, hoping for some kind of positive reaction from him. He was usually quick to jump on any sexual innuendo. Not tonight, apparently.

"I'm sorry. I know you have stuff going on. I should've been more considerate."

Brooke blew out a breath. Clearly, they needed to talk. "Will you be by later?"

Asher shook his head slowly. "Gracie is staying with me

tonight to give Mom and Joel space for their wedding night. I can't leave her alone all night."

Brooke didn't point out that Grace was sixteen and mature enough to stay by herself. She didn't blame him for wanting to stay with her, but now she knew for certain they had a problem. She just wished she knew what she'd done to upset him.

"No, you're right. I understand. And I'll probably be up late incorporating the pictures I took tonight into the pitch I'm giving tomorrow anyway."

"Great. We'll hook up tomorrow then, after your meeting? I'll come by your suite."

Oh. Oh, God.

Brooke's stomach bottomed out. *Hook up.* The words were like a snake crawling up her spine, wrapping around her neck and squeezing tight, tight, *tight*.

Those words triggered the lever on the walls she'd let down for him, slamming them back into place. Hard.

That's what she had done. He must suspect she was in love with him and now he was putting on the brakes, distancing himself from her by reminding her that he didn't do relationships. He *hooked up.*

"Yeah, sure. Tomorrow. Sounds good." Her voice sounded hollow to her own ears.

He leaned down and pressed a soft kiss on her lips. "I'll miss you tonight."

Of course he would. Because that meant they wouldn't have sex.

"Me, too."

"Do you want me to walk you back to your suite?"

She couldn't bare it. "I'll be all right. You should stay with your family. Important day and all."

149

He caressed a thumb over her cheek. "Promise you won't use the trail? It's dark."

His natural protective instincts made it harder for her to keep the tears at bay. She had to get out of there. Now.

"I promise."

"Okay, then. Don't stay up all night working. You're ready. You'll be great tomorrow."

The fact that he didn't even bother to argue with her about walking back to her suite alone in the dark told her everything she needed to know.

Nothing had changed. He warned her he wasn't interested in anything long term, and she hadn't listened. She thought after the night of the fight with Brett that things were different between them. That the drama of what happened on the beach had brought them closer somehow.

Fuck that. She thought he'd changed his mind about being with her. She'd convinced herself that they would leave the island a couple.

She was so stupid.

Brooke forced her expression to stay passive, refusing to let the tears fall where he could see. She'd done exactly what she'd wanted to avoid. She opened her heart to him— again—and he didn't want it—again. Only now she wasn't just losing Asher. She was losing Ellen, Grace, and Joel, too. The family she'd always dreamed of having.

ASHER FOLLOWED Gracie into his suite.

"First dibs on the bathroom," she yelled and took off running, the duffle bag on her shoulder bouncing against her side.

Asher chuckled to himself. He went straight to the

balcony and opened the doors. The room felt stuffy, cramped. Or maybe that was just his head.

He'd been replaying his childhood over and over, looking for clues. His parents had done a damn fine job shielding him from the shit that went down, but the more he thought on it, the more he put the pieces together. The drinking, the late nights, the time away from home.

It amazed him how two people could live through the exact same moment and have two completely different stories to tell. Perspective was a funny thing. Now that he had some, he needed to figure out what that meant for his future with Brooke. He was still struggling with the idea of jumping in with both feet—old habits die hard—but damn, he wanted to.

He couldn't help but imagine he and Brooke on a beach somewhere, standing together as his mom and Joel had. Holding hands and declaring their love in a way that made her eyes glisten.

Asher had never seen anything more beautiful than his girl today as she listened to his mom and Joel commit their lives to each other. He tried to pay attention to the words, but in truth he spent more time trying to memorize Brooke's face and the achingly sweet joy she seemed unable to contain.

This whole being in love thing was throwing him for a loop. It was as if the conversation with his mom last night had given the emotion permission to take root. Taking solace in Brooke's warm body afterward was like dousing those roots with fucking Miracle Gro, and the shit was tossing out branches left and right. He couldn't keep up.

He'd never told a woman, other than his mom and Gracie, that he loved her. The idea scared the shit out of him. Did he just blurt it out or try to make it a special event?

Christ. He didn't have the first idea what he was doing. No wonder his mom warned him not to mess things up, because at this rate, the odds weren't looking to lean in his favor.

"I don't need a babysitter. You can go, you know."

Gracie came back into the room, fresh-faced and dressed in shorts and a top, both with cartoon kittens all over them. She curled into the corner of the couch and tugged a light blanket over her legs.

Ash dropped his suit jacket over the back of a chair and emptied his pockets onto the table. "Go where? This is my room."

"Don't you want to hang out with Brooke tonight?"

Yeah, he did. He wanted to talk to her about everything, but how could he when he was still trying to wrap his head around what he was feeling?

"She's got work to finish before her meeting tomorrow, and I want to hang out with my little sis. I'm gonna go change. Find a movie for us to watch. No chick flicks, though. I need guns and explosions."

When he came back, he was surprised to see the television was dark.

"What's up? Couldn't find anything you wanted to watch?"

"What's going on with you and Brooke?"

Asher sank onto the couch, dropping his head back. "Why do you ask?"

"It seems like you like her."

He rolled his head to look at his sister. "Do you have a point?"

"I was just wondering what she was to you."

She's my everything.

"Not that it's any of your business, but she's important to me."

"I figured, since you've never once introduced me to a girl. I was beginning to think you were gay."

Asher laughed. "I'm as hetero as they come. Trust me on that one."

"So, why haven't I ever met any of your girlfriends?"

"Because I've never had one. What's with all the questions?"

Gracie stretched out her leg and shoved his knee. "Because you're my brother and I feel like I hardly know you. I know you weren't gone all that long this last time, but you're different this week. You seem, I dunno, happier, I guess. I was curious if Brooke was the reason."

And that's how he, Asher Michael Dillon, a thirty-two-year-old Navy SEAL, fell into discussing his relationship with his sixteen-year-old sister.

"I haven't given it much thought, but if I seem happier, I would say Brooke has something to do with it, yeah."

"But then today you were all weird."

"Weird, how?"

"You didn't seem happy she was there. You were scowling at her during the ceremony."

"I was not scowling at her." Was he? He remembered the sun was bright, so he had to squint to make out the freckles he loved so much. "I was just looking at her."

Gracie snorted. "Whatever. You were scowling. And then you introduced her to everyone as Brooke."

Asher got up and went to the bar, where he poured a liberal amount of Blanton's into a glass. He drank down the shot and poured another. "So? That's her name. How did you expect me to introduce her?"

"A guy who's with a woman would usually introduce her as his girlfriend."

Yeah, and that guy should sac up and have the important discussion with his woman so he could actually claim the right to that title.

"We haven't had the whole exclusivity discussion yet."

"Why not?"

"Jesus, you're pushy." He tossed her the remote. "Put on a movie. I'm done with this discussion."

"I'm just saying, I can't speak for Brooke, but most women like to be acknowledged. If I were dating a guy and he acted like I was some random person in his life instead of his girlfriend, I'd be pissed. I might even break up with him."

Asher swallowed another gulp of bourbon. He'd been so far up in his own head today that he hadn't even realized how Brooke might read into his behavior. And he'd let her walk back to her suite alone. He was dying to go with her, but he knew if he did, he'd never leave and she wouldn't get her work done.

At least they had another week together on the island. After her meeting was over tomorrow, he'd take her somewhere they could talk and he would lay his cards on the table.

This time, he was going all in.

14

BROOKE'S CELL phone woke her with a start. She knew where they stood now, but she couldn't keep her stupid heart from fluttering at the thought that it could be Asher calling. Of course, then she remembered they hadn't traded cell numbers. There hadn't been any need. They were in a tropical paradise. Neither one of them had carried their phones while they were exploring the islands. Not to mention they'd spent pretty much every minute together, so she'd forgotten to ask for his number.

Not that you'll need it now.

Brooke rubbed the sleep from her eyes and glanced at the caller ID. She groaned out loud.

Sandra Davenport, the display read.

Damn it all. Her boss was the last person she needed to talk to this morning. She was exhausted from lack of sleep, she hadn't had her tea yet, and her mood was for shit.

Sandra hadn't bothered her all week, a fact that would normally have concerned her had she not been distracted. A radio-silent Sandra was never a good thing.

"Hello?" Brooke sat up straighter and smoothed down

her hair as if the woman was standing in front of her instead of thousands of miles away.

"Are you still asleep? Need I remind you that you are not on vacation? You're supposed to be working."

Sandra's voice had the effect of nails on a chalkboard, causing a shudder to race down Brooke's spine. The time on the bedside table indicated it was nine in the morning. Her meeting with Gregory wasn't until ten-thirty.

"I have been working. I finished the preliminary proposal for the campaign last night," Brooke told her. "I have a meeting with Mr. Meeks later this morning to pitch my ideas and I know he's going to love them. There's nothing to worry about." Brooke had put her heart and soul into selling the couples angle for the resort. *Literally.* "Everything is under control, Sandra."

"Everything is *not* under control. I haven't seen this so-called pitch, and in light of recent events, I'm not sure I trust you to handle this account."

"Recent events?" What was she talking about?

"Give me your suite number."

"I'm sorry, what?"

"I'm in the lobby and the desk won't give me your suite number. I want to see what you've done before you take it to the client. I am your boss, in case you've forgotten. I'm responsible for you. Give me your suite number."

Brooke rattled off the numbers as if her mouth was on autopilot. Sandra was *there*? That couldn't be good.

"I'll be right over," Sandra snipped and the line went dead.

Brooke tossed her phone onto the mattress and bolted for the bathroom. Her hair was stiff from day-old hairspray, but there was no time for a shower. She didn't even bother with a brush. She piled the curls she'd created for the wedding yesterday into a ponytail and slipped a wide head-band around her head. She quickly brushed her teeth with one hand while she raced around the bedroom, pulling clothes and underthings out of drawers.

By the time Sandra knocked on the door, Brooke was dressed, but nowhere near ready.

Everything is going to be fine. You're good at your job, otherwise you wouldn't be here.

Brooke plastered a smile on her face and opened the door.

"Sandra," she said as the woman pushed past her and into the room. "I didn't know you were coming. When did you get in?"

Sandra Davenport was a shrew in every sense of the word. She was in her early forties. Small in stature with hair the color of, well, a shrew. Her nose was bladed and long, far too small for her round face. Her wide set eyes were made bigger by thick, horn-rimmed glasses. Her lips had a permanent curve to the south, as if she had no reason to smile. Ever. And she dressed like someone twice her age, all paisley prints and cardigans.

"It's not your business to know what I'm doing, but I arrived yesterday afternoon." Sandra's face scrunched as she scrutinized Brooke from head to toe. "You look terrible. Are you hungover? Your eyes are all puffy and red."

Because I was up most of the night working, and when I wasn't doing that, I was trying to come to terms with where things are with Asher, which is nowhere, you annoying, nosey bitch.

"I'm not hungover, Sandra. As you stated, I'm here to work, not play."

Sandra sniffed. "Yes, well. That's not what I hear."

"What does that mean?"

"It means I've been talking with the client. Imagine my surprise to learn there wasn't one, but two incidents here at the resort involving you and some man Mr. Meeks claimed to be your boyfriend."

She should've known Sandra would find out about what happened with Brett. "Neither of those incidents were my fault. There was a young man who was harassing me. Both times he got out of line."

"Yes, well, I'm sure you can understand our concern. You represent the Woodson Bellamy Agency and it doesn't look good for the company when one of its employees can't stay out of trouble. And when you're on the client's dime, no less."

Sandra glanced over to where Brooke's company-issued laptop sat on the table. "You say you're ready for the pitch?"

"Yes."

Brooke forced her feet to stay put as Sandra went to the table. Sandra bent down, her hand working the mouse as she apparently flipped through the slides Brooke had stayed up half the night creating. After what felt like hours, Sandra pushed the laptop closed and gathered it close to her chest.

"I'll take this," she said.

Brooke's heart stopped. "Wait. What are you doing? I need that for my meeting."

"You won't be attending the meeting."

"I have to attend. It's my pitch. Those are my ideas. You can't—"

"I can and I will. As of right now, I am taking over the account. And in light of your recent behavior, I have the support of the agency's partners, so don't bother fighting me on this."

Her recent ... oh the *nerve* of this woman. Brooke picked up her phone. She wasn't taking Sandra's word for it. Not this time. "If you have their support, then you won't mind if I call to verify?"

"By all means. Then you can personally explain how you've been spending your time this week." Sandra's smile was one of pure satisfaction. "Oh, that's right. I know what you've been doing on company time. Mr. Meeks tells me you and your male companion were having quite a time on the islands. Romantic dinners, private boat tours, lounging on the beach. He remarked what a lovely couple the two of you make."

"I can explain if you'll only—"

"I expect we will see more of this boyfriend of yours? Will he pop into the office to take you to lunch? Attend the agency Christmas party?"

"Gregory—Mr. Meeks—wanted to focus on promoting the new couples resort that will open next year." Brooke said, proud of herself for remaining calm. "Since he brought me here to experience the resort firsthand anyway, he thought it would be beneficial for me to do so as part of a couple."

"So, you went down to the beach and picked the first man you saw?"

"No. I've known Asher for years." Just saying his name made her heart hurt. "Running into him was a complete coincidence. He's here on vacation with his family." And she really needed to stop talking. "It's kind of a long story."

"I'm not interested in hearing any stories." Sandra crossed her arms. "Is this man your boyfriend or not? A simple yes or no will clear up this whole matter."

Would it? It seemed either way she answered, Sandra would find fault. And there was nothing *simple* when it came to her relationship with Asher.

If Sandra had shown up a day earlier, Brooke would've

said yes, without a doubt, Asher Dillon was indeed her boyfriend. He had been for the last week, in every sense of the word. A day earlier and Brooke would've taken Sandra to meet him, confident she would take one look at them together and realize the truth.

That they were in love.

But, that wasn't the truth, was it? Asher wasn't in love. He wasn't her boyfriend. Not now, not ever. He was with her because of proximity, and because of the outstanding sex they had together.

She was his vacation hook-up.

"No. No, he's not."

Sandra nodded and Brooke wanted to slap the arrogant smile from her face.

"So, you purposely deceived the client."

"It was nothing more than a misunderstanding."

"That you did nothing to rectify. Is that correct?"

Brooke gave in to the sigh ready to let loose in her throat. "I'll admit, I should have explained the situation, but I still don't see what the big deal is. No one was hurt. The client wanted me to experience the couples side of things, and I did." Then she created a kick ass campaign that it appeared she was going to lose.

"The big deal is you misrepresented yourself to a client and got yourself a nice little vacation out of the deal." She snorted with disgust. "Obviously, Brooke, I can't have an advertising executive on my team who lies to her clients to gain favor. How am I ever supposed to trust you now?"

Brooke's hold on her temper broke. "I've worked my ass off for Woodson Bellamy for close to nine years. My work should stand on its own. I've created some of the most successful advertising campaigns the agency has ever produced."

Sandra's brow went up. "Did you?" she asked, and Brooke knew she was screwed. The higher-ups only knew what Sandra wanted them to know.

Brooke had let it happen. She hadn't fought for herself or her work because she hadn't wanted to rock the boat. She was so afraid of losing her steady income that she'd allowed this woman to walk all over her. And all for naught, apparently. She knew what was coming and braced herself for the impact.

Sandra raised her chin. "This should not come as a shock, but you're fired. Effective immediately. Pack your things, Brooke. I've booked you a seat on the morning flight out. It leaves in less than an hour. I've already called you a cab."

Direct. Hit.

ASHER LIFTED the fork full of pancakes to his mouth as he watched Gregory Meeks and a woman he didn't recognize walk into the restaurant. He shoved in the bite, then checked his watch. Ten-fifteen. Gregory's meeting with Brooke was at ten-thirty. He wasn't sure where they were meeting, but he didn't want to intrude if they were meeting there. Brooke needed to know he respected her space, as much as he'd love to watch her work.

He couldn't wait to see her. His bed felt empty and cold last night without her next to him. They had a lot of shit to work out. He wasn't naive or stupid. It wasn't going to be easy. He was entering completely new territory. He was bound to fuck some shit up, but for the first time in his life, he looked forward to the challenge.

He finished his breakfast and stood to leave. The woman

with Meeks had a laptop open on the table. As he walked by, Asher recognized the people in the photo on the screen.

What the hell?

Before he knew what he was doing, Asher walked over.

"Hey, Meeks," he greeted.

Gregory's gaze shifted from him to the woman and back, looking uncomfortable as hell.

"Sorry to interrupt. I couldn't help but notice that picture—"

The woman slammed the laptop closed. "I'm sorry. That's proprietary information."

"If that picture is of who I think it is, then you're damn right." The woman's uppity tone got under his skin. Asher ignored her protests as he reached over, spun the laptop to face him and opened the screen. There, in the center, was one of the full-page advertisements Brooke had created featuring his mom and Joel at their wedding.

"Where did you get that? Where's Brooke?" This was the biggest opportunity of her career. There was no way she would've missed it.

"We are in the middle of a meeting," the woman said.

Asher continued to ignore her. He addressed Meeks instead. "You wanna tell me why this woman is here pitching Brooke's hard work, instead of Brooke herself?"

"I don't know what you're talking about," the woman said. "This campaign wasn't created by any one person. It was created by the Woodson Bellamy Agency."

Asher crossed his arms. "And you are?"

"I'm Sandra Davenport, senior advertising executive."

"Well, Ms. Davenport, I can tell you without a shadow of a doubt that what you just said is a load of bullshit. Brooke Ramsey created that ad all on her own, because I watched her do it."

"Ms. Davenport," Meeks cut in. "This is Brooke's boyfriend. The man I was telling you about. Asher Dillon."

Sandra smirked. "Boyfriend, huh? That's not what Brooke said."

Asher ground his teeth. Oh, he knew who the woman was. She was Brooke's boss. The one who had it out for Brooke.

"Where is she?"

"I'd say by now she's well on her way back to San Diego." Asher couldn't move. He couldn't breathe.

Brooke was gone? Why the fuck would she just leave?

"What did you do?" he practically snarled. If Sandra had been a man, she'd be spitting teeth right about now.

"I had to let her go. I did what was best for the client and my company."

Asher cursed. Loudly. He dropped his knuckles against the table and leaned in. "Let me be very clear. Those photos belong to me and my family. We do not give our consent to you or your agency to use the photos. If you do use them, we won't hesitate to sue you for copyright infringement. It might also interest you to know the man in those photographs is Navy SEAL Commander Joel Taylor. Trust me when I say you do not want to piss him off.

"And as for you," Asher didn't even try to hide his disgust as he looked down his nose at Sandra. "You better enjoy your job while you have it, because I just made it my personal mission to see you removed from your position."

He didn't know if the top brass at the company would listen to what he had to say, but he damn sure was going to set up a meeting and let them know the kind of person they had managing their employees.

Asher turned to leave. He made it to the lobby before his

knees gave out and he had to sit down on one of the over-sized lounge chairs they had there.

He dropped his head into his hands. What the fuck was he supposed to do now?

Brooke was gone.

"This was not my doing." Asher's head snapped up at Gregory's voice. "I hated to hear what happened. I assure you, I quite enjoyed Ms. Ramsey."

A growl emanated from Asher's throat. "Not what I need to hear right now, Meeks."

"Then how about this. I am fully aware of who did the work on our campaign. From what I've seen so far, Ms. Ramsey captured my vision for the new area perfectly. The unfortunate truth of the matter is we signed a contract with the Woodson Bellamy Agency for this resort."

"You do what you have to do, Meeks, but I meant what I said in there. If I see one ad featuring my parents, or any other photograph Brooke took while on this island, we will take action to stop it."

Gregory nodded. "I understand that, but you didn't let me finish. We signed a contract for the resort here in Grand Turks."

"Yeah, I heard you the first time. What's your point?"

"The point is Ms. Ramsey is very talented and we have five other resorts not under contract." Meeks handed Asher his card. "When you see her, please tell her to give me a call."

As Meeks walked away, Asher reached in his pocket for his phone when it hit him like a battering ram.

Motherfucker. He didn't have her goddamn phone number.

He squeezed the phone in his fist. It was either that or

throw the fucking thing across the lobby, which might make him feel better, but wouldn't help him in the least.

He was going to need his phone to find her. When he did, he would make sure she understood he was in this for the long haul. And then, he'd make goddamn sure she never ran from him again.

15

———

Ten days later

BROOKE WAS A CLICHÉ. She hadn't left her apartment, gotten dressed, or eaten anything except peanut butter from the jar, ramen noodles, and ice cream, since that's all she had readily available after cleaning out her fridge before she left for Grand Turks.

She managed to shower most days, though. Not that it mattered, since she had no one to see and no reason to leave her apartment.

God, she missed Asher. There was an empty place in her chest where her heart used to be. He'd taken a piece of her all those years ago, and this time he finished the job.

She'd tried to come to terms with things, but it seemed her ability to adapt to any situation had abandoned her. Probably because she didn't want to adapt to a life without him.

She was pathetic.

Brooke shuffled into the kitchen to make a cup of tea. At some point in the very near future, she would need to start looking for another job. The money she'd managed to save would get her through for a year, maybe more if she stayed on the peanut butter-ramen-ice cream diet.

Yeah. She really needed to start that online job search. She'd get right on that ... after she had her tea.

She pulled out her favorite flavor and dropped a teabag into a mug. She grabbed the screeching kettle from the stove. A knock on the door startled her and she jumped, spilling boiling water onto the counter, which then splashed down onto the tops of her bare feet.

Brooke yelped and dropped the kettle into the sink, out of harm's way.

The knock turned into a pounding. "Brooke! Are you all right? What happened? Open the door."

Her chest constricted as the voice penetrated the haze that had fallen over her life. Without thought she was pulling open the door and Asher was there. He looked amazing in dark jeans and a light-colored, short-sleeved Henley. His tan was a little darker, as was the look in his eyes as he took her in.

"What happened? I heard you cry out."

"I spilled some hot water on myself. I'm fine. How did you find me? I never told you exactly where I lived."

"I'm a US Navy SEAL with high level security clearance, baby. The question you should be asking is why it took me so long."

"What are you doing here, Asher?"

"Got important things to say." He stepped into her apartment and pushed the door closed. "And you need to hear them."

A puff of laughter escaped her lips before she could catch it. "What makes you think I want to hear anything you have to say?"

He walked toward her, one slow step at a time. For every step, she took one of her own, backing away from him.

"You've got to stop running from me, Brooke."

"You don't have to do this. I get it."

His eyes narrowed. "What do you get?"

"You disappeared from my life, Ash. You're not back in it by choice. You're in it by chance. You aren't under any obligation to stay."

His lips flattened. "I got on a plane three days after you left Grand Turk because I was miserable without you. That was a choice. I've spent the last week searching for you. That was a choice. I'm here now. That is a fucking choice."

Her back hit the wall and she realized she had nowhere left to go.

She held her breath as Asher slipped his palm around the back of her neck and leaned his forehead against hers.

"Maybe we did meet by accident this time, but it was the best fucking thing to ever happen to me. For eight years, I've kept myself closed off, emotionally unavailable to all other women. I might not have realized it at the time, but I did that because they weren't you. Don't you see, baby? All this time I've been waiting, I've been waiting for you."

He captured her mouth and wasted no time deepening the kiss. She tasted his hunger, his anger, and his ... no.

Brooke shoved him back, tears burning her eyelids. "You can't keep doing this to me."

"Doing what?

"You're messing with my head and I can't take it anymore. I don't know what you want. I let myself believe things had changed between us. Then the day of the wedding you closed yourself off again. You were pulling away from me."

"Ah, Brooke. Is that what you think?"

"What would you call it?"

"I'd call it love."

She froze, wondering if she'd heard him correctly. "What?"

"You heard me. I had just come to terms with the fact that I love you and there was no way in hell I was ever going to let you go. I'm gonna ask that you cut me a little slack for that day. When a guy's whole philosophy on life gets flushed down the toilet, it takes a minute for his head to catch up. Can you forgive me?"

"You ... you love me?"

"More than life itself. I've been through the wringer the last week and a half. I couldn't stand the thought that I might've lost you again. And on that note, where's your phone?"

She glanced toward the coffee table where her phone sat. Asher followed her gaze. He marched over and picked up it. He tapped the screen and turned it so she could unlock it with her thumb print.

She watched as his fingers moved over the screen. When he was finished, he once again showed her the screen. He'd added his contact information. Under *Name* he typed *Asher Dillon*. Under *Title* there was a single word. *Mine.*

There was really no way to misinterpret that.

He hit the call button and Asher's phone buzzed. His fingers moved as be typed something onto the screen. When he was finished, he held it out.

It was her contact information.

Name: Brooke Ramsey

Title: Mine

"Gracie said women like to be acknowledged, and this is the first in a long line of ways I plan to claim you."

Brooke heart was full but her brain was still suspicious.

"Are you trying to tell me that in less than two weeks you've conquered your fear of relationships?"

"Not at all. I'm fucking terrified. But, I'm here and I love you. I want this. I want *you*. No more running."

"Are you staying in the Navy?"

"I'd like to, yes. We've got six months to decide. We'll figure it out. No more running."

"So, what happens when you get deployed? Who's to say you won't get to wherever you're going and decide the whole thing is more hassle than it's worth?"

"*Never*. I'm all in, baby. And don't ever call us a hassle again. We are *everything*."

"Full disclosure. I should tell you I don't have a job."

"I know. I met your former boss the morning you left the resort." He reached into his pocket, dug out a card, and handed it to her. "Gregory wants to talk to you about his other resorts."

"Really?"

He nodded. "It seems to me you could write your own ticket with any agency in town with an account like that in your pocket. And it seems there's an opening for a senior account executive at your old agency." He winked at her. "You might want to give them a call."

"Asher. What did you do?"

"I had my girl's back. You better get used to it, baby."

She stared at him for a long moment. There was no way she could deny the love she felt for him was reflected back at her through his eyes. He looked determined, hopeful, and yeah, even scared. Her big, bad-ass Navy SEAL, who wasn't afraid of anything, had put his heart on the line for the first time.

She would spend the rest of her life making sure he'd never regret coming for her.

"I'm all in, too. I love you, Asher. I've always loved you." she said, laughing when the air left his lungs in a rush of air.

"Thank Christ." He pulled her into his arms and swung her around. He took her mouth with a quick, hard kiss. "It's you and me against the world now. Whatever life throws our way, we will handle it. Together. No more running."

Brooke grinned, happier than she would've ever thought possible.

"No more running? Are you absolutely sure?"

"Brooke," he warned, dragging out her name.

She went up on her toes and put her mouth against his ear. "What if I want to run to the bedroom?"

Asher stiffened, his whole body going hard and taut. He growled, low and deep. He spun her around and smacked her ass. Hard.

"In that case, I'll give you a head start."

MORE SEALS IN PARADISE

Hot SEAL, Salty Dog by Elle James
Hot Seal, S*x on the Beach by Delilah Devlin
Hot Seal, Dirty Martini by Cat Johnson
Hot SEAL, Red Wine by Becca Jameson
Hot Seal, Cold Beer by Cynthia D'Alba
Hot Seal, Rusty Nail by Teresa Reasor
Hot Seal, Single Malt by Kris Michaels
Hot Seal, Black Coffee by Cynthia D'Alba

When a Texas belle is cheated on by
a second man, she resolves to have it
their way--hook up and move on, no
regrets. It's just that the guy she chooses
is hotter than the Texas sun, and
different than any other man she's
known. Can a jaded beauty and a lonely
ex-military sniper make it work?

Please turn the page for a preview
of book one in Parker Kincade's award-
winning Martin Family series.

One Night Stand

PROLOGUE

"HONESTLY AMANDA, he wasn't good enough for you," Samantha said as she tossed back a shot of cinnamon whiskey.

"You never complained about him before."

"What was I supposed to say? 'Hey, I think your boyfriend is a douche'? Yeah, right." Sam snorted. "That would have gone over well."

Another shot.

"That's exactly what you should have said," Amanda huffed, but she knew Sam was right. Dammit. "Are you here for moral support or to get drunk?"

"The two have to be mutually exclusive?"

Amanda snickered at her best friend.

"I'm the one who got cheated on, and you're the one getting drunk. How does that work again?"

"Wasn't planning on doing it alone." Sam winked as she sailed a tiny tumbler across the table to her.

Amanda poured the fiery liquid into the glass and took her shot. She shuddered, embracing the warmth that infused her body and mind, and she relaxed for the first time in days.

"So"—Sam waved a finger at her—"do the three horsemen of the apocalypse know about it yet?"

Her brothers. Sweet Jesus, when they found out it was going to get ugly. And potentially bloody. Those boys did love a good fight. She almost felt sorry for Scott. Almost.

"God, no. I have enough to deal with without adding those three to the mix. They seem to think their sole purpose in life is to defend my honor." She rolled her eyes. "What they end up doing is just irritating the crap out of me with their Neanderthal bullshit. I don't need to be bailing their asses out of jail, again I might add, because they've got testosterone poisoning."

Amanda considered her friend. "You know they hate it when you call them that."

"All the more reason, my friend. All the more reason." The gleam in Sam's eye was sinfully wicked as she raised her shot in silent toast.

"What the hell is wrong with me?" Amanda blurted, hating the pitiful twang of her voice. "I'm getting a serious complex here. I mean, what am I supposed to do now?"

She stared into her empty shot glass like she'd find the answer magically spelled out at the bottom.

"Call the horsemen. Set up the ass kicking. Sell tickets." Sam giggled like a five-year-old.

Amanda narrowed her eyes, letting a sound of pure frustration pass her lips.

"Fine." Sam slammed her empty glass on the table so hard it shook. "Want to know what I think? I think you need to get laid."

Amanda's head fell back on the edge of her chair. "That's your answer for everything."

"Maybe not the answer to everything, but it sure would help you get your mojo back." Sam's tone became serious. "Listen, Amanda, you need to get away. Take a vacation. Find a gorgeous stranger and have wild monkey sex with him. Be spontaneous." Sam smiled at her as she refilled their glasses.

Amanda tossed back her shot. "I fail to see how that's going to help me."

Sam gave her a droll stare. "Of course you fail to see how it will help. That's precisely why you need to do it."

1
___

AMANDA MARTIN PULLED her car into the parking lot. She stared at the small building that served as the local watering hole before she turned off the ignition and slumped back in her seat.

Cheated on again. This must be some kind of record.

So far, the only two serious relationships she'd had were colossal failures. It took her first ex all of six months to jump into another bed. Well, that she knew of anyway. Chances were he'd cheated long before coming clean, telling her he just couldn't see himself with her forever. As if she were deficient or something.

She'd convinced herself that Scott, her most recent of disasters, was different. He was charismatic and sweet. Okay, so the sex wasn't mind-blowing, but they'd had it on a regular basis. So what the hell happened?

She'd caught the bastard in bed with another woman.

His secretary. *Jesus.*

She snorted in disgust. She didn't know if she was madder that he'd cheated on her or that he'd turned her into a cliché. She figured she should be way more pissed off about the cheating. The fact that she wasn't meant she'd wasted the last year of her life on average sex with a guy she didn't really care about. Wouldn't that make her family proud?

And now here she sat in all her pathetic-ness, feeling sorry for herself.

In the parking lot of a bar in Nowhere, Texas.

What the hell am I doing?

Amanda liked the stability of a steady relationship. The idea of bouncing from man to man just didn't appeal to her. But maybe Sam was right. Maybe it was time for her to change her ways. Shake things up. Maybe a one-night stand was just what she needed. After all, she was young and relatively attractive.

She could do this, couldn't she?

Right. Time to buck up or shut up.

The gravel crunched under her boots as she made her way across the parking lot. Two cars flanked the front door and she breathed a sigh of relief that the place wouldn't be overly crowded. She tried to act casual, stopping just inside the door to let her eyes adjust to the light—or lack thereof.

The smell of stale beer and peanuts hung heavy in the darkened interior. Tables were spread around the perimeter of a small, open area she assumed was used for dancing. The jukebox belted out an old Hank Williams tune while its neon glow permeated the light haze of cigarette smoke. The other side sported a shuffleboard table and a pool table, along with several stray chairs turned this way and that. The bar ran the length of the back, with doors on each end, one marked *Private* and the other indicating restrooms beyond. She sauntered toward the bar, the butterflies in her stomach the only betrayal of her nervousness.

Two men played pool, swaying and obviously drunk,

and eyed her curiously as she slid onto a barstool. They both wore jeans that had seen better days, worn through the knees and streaked with dirt. Their grease-stained T-shirts and ball caps made her wonder if they'd rolled out from underneath a truck before walking in here.

The taller of the two offered her a calculating smile, showing off the yellow stain of his teeth.

Maybe this wasn't such a good idea.

"What'll ya have, miss?" The bartender asked, keeping a purposeful eye on the two playing pool.

"Whiskey. Straight up." She'd gone for confident, but ended up just sounding cheesy. All she needed was to fist bump the bar and she'd be in an old Western.

"Whiskey. Right," the bartender said with humor in his voice. "You're not from around here, are you?"

Thank you, Captain Obvious.

"No, I'm just here for the week. I've got a place not far from here."

"I see," he said, raising his brows in surprise. "So, what brings you to our fine establishment?"

He slid a drink to her.

"Fine, huh?" Amanda looked around. "Guess I was lucky to find a seat," she joked.

He flashed her a gorgeous smile. Stretching his arms out, he indicated to the rest of the room. "You just missed the rush. Ten minutes ago we were packed to the gills."

The mischievous gleam in his eye told her he was lying. He was working for what would probably be the only tip he saw all night. Amanda laughed, swirling the amber liquid around in her glass before taking a sip.

"Name's Jacob, but most folks just call me Jake."

"Nice to meet you, Jake."

He considered her a moment. "You got a name?"

She laughed again, blushing. She really needed to work on her flirting skills. "Amanda. My name is Amanda."

"Nice to meet you, Amanda." His gaze darted to the two men slowly approaching the bar.

"Yeah, Amanda," the taller of the two said, "it's very nice to meet ya." He took the bar stool to her left while his buddy chuckled and stumbled to the seat on her right. They stunk of alcohol and cigarettes, the combination making her eyes water.

Oh, this was a very bad idea.

"No trouble in here tonight, boys," Jake warned. "Back off."

"Aw, we don't want no trouble, Jake. We just wanna talk to the li'l lady here." The man to her left reached out to touch her hair.

"Let's *not* with the touching, big man." Amanda veered away. There were some things she wouldn't stand for. Invasion of her personal space was definitely one of them.

"That's enough, Clete." Jake crossed his arms over his chest. "Not gonna say it again."

Amanda slammed back the rest of her whiskey, ignoring the fact that it fried a hole in her stomach as she signaled Jake for another. "Hey, Clete"—she looked him dead in the eye—"how about I buy you and your buddy a beer and you go back to your game of pool?"

Then I can get the hell out of here.

"You're a mite more in'eresting than playin' pool, sweet thang." Clete weaved toward her.

Amanda boldly pushed at the man's chest. "While that may be so, I'm much more interested in being left alone."

"She's got a mouth on her, that's for sure." Clete's buddy leaned in until she could feel his breath on her neck.

Amanda's blood began to boil. She didn't need this shit.

She was here to blow off some steam, not be harassed by a couple of smart-assed drunks.

"Get. Off." Amanda shoved her elbow into the man behind her. Having grown up with three brothers, she had no doubt she could defend herself, but she had enough common sense to know when it was time to go. Sliding off her bar stool, she reached into her pocket for cash to pay for her drink. She noticed Jake moving toward her side of the bar.

"Where you goin', li'l lady?"

She felt a hand slide over her ass. Amanda froze.

Oh, hell no.

Before she could stop herself, she balled up her fist and swung around hard. She made contact with the man's jaw with a sickening *crack*.

"Listen up, fuckwit," Amanda spat as she watched Clete fall from his bar stool and land on the floor with a thud. A mixture of adrenaline and fear caused her voice to quiver. "I told you not to touch me."

She flexed her hand. Yep. That was gonna hurt in the morning.

Jake was there in a heartbeat, placing himself between her and the men. Better late than never, she supposed. His palms were up to each side, his dark eyes darting between them as if he wasn't sure who he needed to protect from whom.

Clete was still on the floor, his buddy laughing over him. "She sure showed you, Clete," his friend slurred.

"Shut up, Ernie." Clete glared at Amanda, retribution burning in his eyes.

That's it.

She'd thought she would come here to unwind with a drink or two. Maybe find a gorgeous guy to have sex with.

Now she was pissed, her hand hurt like the devil, and all she wanted was her couch and an ice pack. And maybe to kick Sam's ass for talking her into this little fiasco in the first place. And maybe another bottle of whiskey.

She wondered if Jake would sell her a bottle for the road.

A voice, low and full of menace, drifted from behind her just seconds before she felt him. Well, not so much felt as sensed. Like a rabbit would sense it was about to become coyote kibble. His heat penetrated her back. Amanda stiffened as she felt his hands move over the skin of her arms, hovering but not actually touching.

"What the fuck, Jake?" he growled.

Amanda spun to look at the man behind her and came face-to-face with his pecs.

Oh. Wow.

Her gaze roamed upward. He was well over six feet tall. Over six feet of powerful male. His black T-shirt strained against the pressure of containing all those muscles. Before she could stop herself, she leaned forward to take in his scent. Her head spun as the dizzying combination of leather and sandalwood drifted through her. She turned away before he noticed the heat that flooded her cheeks.

"It's under control, Joe," Jake snapped.

Joe pointed at the two drunkards. "You have one minute to get your shit and get out of my bar." He gently, cautiously, touched her arm. "Are you okay, slugger?" His mouth was so close to her ear she could feel his breath on her neck. His husky voice reverberated down her spine. The heady combination caused a reflexive shiver to run through her body.

His eyes narrowed dangerously on Clete. Clearly mistaking her reaction for fear, he growled, "Make that thirty seconds." He eased protectively in front of her.

Clete swore an oath as he pushed to his feet and stumbled toward the door. His friend followed close behind. Joe led her back to the stool she'd just vacated. "Here ... sit." His large hands engulfed her shoulders as he bent to look into her eyes. "Slugger?"

Amanda got her first good look at him. Her mind went blank. A strong jaw that narrowed slightly at the tip of his chin sported a dark five o'clock shadow. His lips were red and full and entirely too inviting. Jet-black hair fell in disarray around his face, thick locks waving across his forehead. And he had the bluest eyes she'd ever seen. Eyes that were narrowed in concern for her.

She cleared her throat. "Amanda," she rasped. Okay, so she *could* talk. Sort of. "I'm Amanda."

"Amanda."

Good Lord!

Her name on his lips was like a caress that went all the way to her core. She went instantly wet. She clenched her legs together and took a deep breath.

"You okay, Amanda?" he prodded.

"Yes, I'm fine." *Aroused*. "Just pissed off." She shot a glare at Jake. "And where the hell were you?"

Jake's jaw clenched. "What do you mean—"

"Shut the hell up, Jake. What you need to do is thank your lucky stars you're my brother or I'd be kicking your ass all over this county, get me?"

Amanda couldn't hold in her surprise. "Wait. You"—she took advantage of the opportunity to peruse his delicious male body from head to booted toe—"are related to him?" She nodded toward Jake.

"Look Amanda, I'm sorry," Jake said. "No excuses. I should have thrown them out the minute they approached you. I don't know what got into them tonight. Normally they're harmless."

Her anger immediately deflated. "It's not your fault, Jake. I should have just walked away." She sighed. "I know better." She looked back to Joe. God, he took her breath away. Jake was cute, sure, in that boyish I-wanna-make-out-with-you-in-the-back-of-a-Chevy way. But this man, with his long legs encased in tight, faded jeans that seemed to bulge in all the appropriate places, was a work of art. Carved by the gods to bring women to their knees. And speaking of knees, the package he was sporting certainly made her want to get on hers.

Focus, Amanda.

He gave her a half smile and extended his hand. "I'm Joe. Owner of this bar and"—he waved his hand at his brother —"the better looking of the two."

Jake snorted something that sounded a lot like "You wish," as he brought around a towel full of ice for her hand.

She reached to return the greeting, remembering too late the punch she'd thrown. Joe seemed well aware of her discomfort, gently cupping her hand in both of his.

"Vicious right hook you got there, Mandy."

"I have brothers," she said. As though that explained everything. At some point she'd regain her brain function. As soon as he stopped looking at her. And touching her.

Oh God, please don't stop touching me.

"Brothers who taught their sister how to fight?" His eyes danced with amusement.

"Overbearing, overprotective, and over-in-my-face brothers who wanted to make sure I'd never be taken advantage of." She smiled sweetly. "I'm sorry. I didn't mean to cause trouble."

Joe drew back in surprise. "I'm not entirely sure what

happened before I came in, but I'm fairly certain it wasn't your fault." He reached out and tucked her hair behind her ear. "Wanna tell me what happened?" He took the ice pack from Jake and placed it delicately across the back of her hand.

She hissed as the rough towel scraped her sensitive knuckles. "It's no big deal. Couple of drunks getting handsy. It wasn't anyone's fault. It happened so fast. I overreacted."

"I'm sure you didn't overreact." Joe's voice turned hard again. "Those two are a pain in my ass." He shared a knowing look with Jake. "And they've just had their last beer here."

"They were almost a pain in my ass, too," she joked. "But I'm good. Won't be the first time I've nursed sore knuckles."

"You fight a lot then, slugger?"

She laughed at that. "Did I mention that I've got *three* brothers?"

He gave her a smile that had her nipples aching and pushing through her T-shirt. She squirmed in her seat, which only served to rub the seam of her jeans harder against her pulsating clit. She bit back a moan. *So this is what it feels like to be aroused to near pain.* She was close to throwing herself at him, audience be damned. Anything to relieve the tension building in her panties.

Joe noticed her distress. She watched as he slowly took stock of her. She knew the minute he saw the pearled buds of her chest, protruding shamelessly for his inspection. His jaw clenched and his back stiffened. She dared a quick glance at his lap. She hoped his back wasn't the only thing that had turned rigid. His eyes narrowed; his nostrils flared as if he could smell her arousal.

She watched in fascination as his gaze turned dark, smoky.

What would it be like to spend the night in the arms of a man like him? What kind of lover would he be? The thought caused her insides to turn to jelly. There was only one way to find out.

"Are you sure you're okay, Mandy?" His voice was hoarse. His fingers were stroking her palm as he continued to hold her injured hand. She desperately wanted him to be stroking her somewhere else.

It's now or never.

"That depends." Amanda gave him a seductive smile. "You wanna get out of here?"

Joe shook his head, his expression filled with genuine confusion.

"Excuse me?"

Amanda felt her face grow hot with embarrassment. This man was a walking god and here she was, Miss Plain-and-Ordinary, propositioning him. What was she thinking?

She stood a little too quickly, causing her bar stool to wobble before righting itself again. "Never mind. Sorry." She threw two twenty-dollar bills on the bar. "This should cover it." She hollered thanks to Jake as she made her way to the door.

"Mandy, wait."

ABOUT THE AUTHOR

USA Today Bestselling author Parker Kincade is known for her award-winning, edge-of-your-seat-sexy romantic suspense, hot and steamy sports romance, and contemporary western romance. She lives in the southern United States where she spends her days spoiling her beloved boxer, enjoying life as a grandparent, and dreaming up sexy alpha men for the next adventure. Learn more about Parker Kincade at www.parkerkincade.com.

To receive an email when Parker releases a new book, sign up for her newsletter!

http://www.parkerkincade.com/newsletter

ALSO BY PARKER KINCADE

The Martin Family
One Night Stand
Shadow of Sin
No Control (Deadly Seven Crossover)
Tempting Montana (Deadly Seven Crossover)
Ties That Burn (TBD)
Midnight Tidings (TBD)

The Deadly Seven
No Control (Martin Family Crossover)
Tempting Montana (Martin Family Crossover)
Saving Kate (TBD)

Game On
Spring Training
Southern Heat
Wild Catch (formerly Dare's Wild: TBD)
Devon's Fall (TBD)

Shadow Maverick Ranch
White Collar Cowboy
Borrowed Cowboy
Cowboy Redeemed

White Collar Wedding (short story)

Shadow Maverick Ranch Boxed Set (Book 1-3)

Short Stories

Devlin

Two of Cups (Love in the Cards Anthology)

Made in the USA
Coppell, TX
14 July 2023

19152790R00121